TOCABAGA 5

THE QUISLINGS & ANDROKTONES

THOMAS H. WARD

TOCABAGA 5:

The Quislings & Androktones

THE TOCABAGA CHRONICLES

by

THOMAS H. WARD

ISBN-13: 978-0692335963

ISBN-10: 069233596X

Transcendent Publishing
www.transcendentpublishing.com

PREFACE

I'm the oldest of three brothers. We grew up fighting bullies and gang members in a tough neighborhood on the south side of Chicago. My Dad one of the most honest men I have known always stressed, tell the truth, and help each other. Never ever be a bully, never steal, and try to protect those who cannot protect themselves. I have always stood up for the people who could not defend themselves. I hate liars and bullies.

I'm Director of Security for Tocabaga Island. I live here along with 556 other Patriots. We are fighting to keep our freedom, keep our homes, and keep our families safe, from the evil forces gone wild. Tocabaga is a sanctuary. If you believe in the Constitution, the Bill of Rights, and are of good moral character you are welcome here. I do not reveal the full names of the people living here in case the Feds happen to come upon these chronicles. Read my story and tell others what has happened here.

We are waiting for you to contact us by email to find out where Tocabaga is located. Sending us an email is your first step to Freedom. There is an email address hidden in these chronicles. Tocabaga is a real location and I will reply.

My name is Jack Gunn, a.k.a. Tocabaga Jack, and these are my chronicles.

INTELLIGENCE BRIEF

Secretly the Federal government, secretly working with the National Security Agency, has developed a new and even more dangerous combat weapon. Now there is an Army of Droids called RCCDs' operated like drones by a controller or droid master sitting in a room far away from the dangers of battle field. In fact they are walking robots that have no brain, no sense of right or wrong, only that of its master controlling this monster.

These Remote Controlled Combat Droids (RCCD) machines can see in daylight or darkness using cameras, radar, and thermal imaging. These android soldiers along with flying drones could be a formidable force even for the Army Rangers. The machines are big standing 8 feet tall at about 1000 pounds. They can carry almost any type of weapon. Droids do not need to eat or sleep. They are dangerous, very dangerous, and offer only death to those who oppose them as they have no heart.

We call these androids "THE HEPHAESTUS ARMY" or "BOTs" for short. We know some day they will come for us. We're getting ready for the battle.

The Army Rangers have a new combat soldier called the TALOS Warriors who also take on the steel monsters of death. The exoskeleton TALOS combat units are used from time to time for extremely dangerous missions. These TALOS units have developed into fully armored protective suits that a soldier steps into, thereby becoming bullet proof.

The TALOS suit is a fully integrated system. It contains computers, sensors, 360 degree camera, and radio antennas to improve the warrior's real-time battlefield information. It has integrated coolers and heaters that can control the temperature inside the suit. It monitors the body temperature, heart rate, and hydration level of the warrior. The suit has an exoskeleton which operates by electrical-hydraulic servo systems which is powered by a new atomic battery pack that can provide energy for one year without a charge. The exoskeleton supports the weight of the suit and the equipment. The hydraulic systems enable the wearer to have amazing strength.

The helmet is round and angled with no flat surfaces so bullets will be defected. It has a small face shield with two eyes. It has a heads-up display with thermal imaging and infrared. The operator can use a computer laser aiming device that never misses a target.

The Army Rangers destroyed 400 Federal Police BOTs that were coming to attack Tocabaga. They also captured two Federal Police Force semi trucks which contained 10 robots in working order. They were being secretly moved under guard to SOCOM HQ for further analysis by the Army. The convoy was attacked and eight Army Rangers are MIA. Dr. Carl Urban, Jr., one of the robot inventors, who came to work for the Army is among those missing.

Jack Gunn has discovered there is a spy living on Tocabaga feeding information to the Federal Police Force. The spy alerted the FPF that the semi trucks were being moved by sending a coded radio message. The coded message was intercepted and Jack needs help to decipher that message. If you can decipher the code email Jack by finding his email address in The Tocabaga Chronicles.

JUNE 27, 2025

I suspected that the spy on Tocabaga was Guy Allen but I couldn't prove it. If he's the spy I would need to terminate him. He's the kind of person who would shoot you in the back. GA is also the type to hold a grudge and he believes in an eye for an eye like I do. I've had many disagreements with him in the past.

Last night Corporal Phillips called me to say that a coded message was sent by a CB radio and he recorded it. I eased my bones out of bed, had a cup of mud, and woke up my crew. We headed for Fort Desoto after a breakfast of fried eggs with fish nuggets. It was 6 am and I was excited to hear the CB message. I was hoping that I would recognize the voice or at least one of us would.

We made a list of suspects yesterday, people we thought were shady.

There's Scotty, a loner who sold real estate in the past. No one knows what he really thinks about the Feds. Scotty works out in the fields helping Maggie with the farming. He's about 45 years old, keeps to himself, and doesn't make any trouble. Scotty carries a small 380 Colt in his pocket.

Chase is also a loner who always agrees with everyone but never offers his own ideas or opinions. We don't know which side he is really on. He's also a farmer and has one or two friends he hangs around with at the local bar. He smokes pot and drinks too much. Chase doesn't carry a gun.

Troy is an out spoken older man around 60 years old. He used to be an Electronics Engineering Professor at USF. Many college professors are liberals, progressive socialists, or maybe even Communists. His Son became Commie years ago and moved to China. He has some weird political views and leans toward being a socialist. I have never seen Troy carry a gun. He does electrical repair work for the island.

Ellen would do anything if it benefited her in some way. She can't be trusted to do anything right so no one likes to work with her. Ellen smokes pot and is a hard drinker. In her younger days she was an exotic dancer and is a good looking woman but has no husband or boy friend. She would date anyone who wore pants. Ellen isn't the sharpest pencil in the box.

Johnny is a Tocabaga fisherman who always goes fishing by himself. Johnny would say one thing one day and then deny he said it the next day. Johnny would lie about it; whether it's intentional or not we don't know. He always carries a gun and he knows how to use it.

The question is which person had a background that exposed them to the Federal Police Force? Who had a chance to make contact with the Feds in the past? If we can find that out then we can check which name shows up on the communication logs or on the bridge sign out log.

We went over the list of persons living here again and found one person we missed. He is one of the most out spoken liberals living on Tocabaga. He comes from long line of Government Union Members. I know he voted for the last President who got us in this mess and he likes the idea of the government controlling everything.

The one thing he doesn't like is giving up his gun to the government. I think that's the only reason why he lives here. He's walking a thin line but he knows Tocabaga is the only safe place to live. His name is Guy Allen but everyone calls him GA for short. GA moved here about 8 years ago from Georgia after his wife died from the flu. He has a distinct southern accent.

GA thinks he is a tough guy and he doesn't take shit from anyone. He stands 5 feet 10 inches tall and is about 180 pounds. He keeps his brown hair cut short and is clean-shaven. He always carries his Colt 45 Commander and I'm sure he wouldn't hesitate to use it. He's assigned to the Tocabaga fishing crew because that's what he likes to do. He does have three friends who more or less think the same type of liberal crap as he does. They always hang around together and I would never trust any of them with my life.

I told my spy hunters to concentrate on GA to see what they could find out. Ron would follow him everywhere he goes for a few days. Tommy would check his car, boat, and house for a CB radio. Jim Bo was back up for Tommy.

I warned my crew to be careful and don't let anyone know they're looking for a spy. I reminded them of the Stand Your Ground Law. I advised them not to take any chances; if their life is in danger shoot first and ask questions later.

"The Stand Your Ground Law states that a person has no duty or other requirement to abandon a place in which he has a right to be, or to give up ground to an assailant. A person is justified in the use of deadly force and does not have a duty to retreat if he or she reasonably believes that such force is necessary to prevent imminent death or great bodily harm to himself or another or to prevent the imminent commission of a forcible felony."

We arrived at the Fort around 7:30 am and went to the radio office. As we walked in Corporal Phillips said, "Good morning Gentlemen," and we all returned the greeting.

"Captain Sessions wants to see you right away." We walked across to the room to Captain's office and knocked on the door.

"Enter," Sessions advised.

"Hello Captain, you wanted to see us," I stated.

"Have a seat Gentlemen. I have some bad news." As we sat down he continued speaking.

"The trucks we sent to SOCOM last night were ambushed near the Dome exit on Route 275. Eight Rangers who were security for that convoy are MIA. We received one short radio message advising they were under attack and then the radio went dead. All we heard was static. We flew drones to the area right away but their video signals were blocked. It leaves me to believe that the BOTs are back."

The Dome was closed years ago and was once called Tropicana Field. It's an old enclosed baseball stadium that is fairly large, seating up to 30,000 people, so it could take up to an hour to search. No one knows what could be inside, but rumor has it that political prisoners are being held there.

"That's not all SOCOM HQ is under attack by a large force and I had to fly the TALOS Warriors there last night to provide re-enforcements."

"How large of a force and who are they?" I asked.

"SOCOM estimates they are facing about two Battalions. It's a combined force consisting of Federal Agents and BOTs."

Generally operational Army Units conform

to the following for man power: Squad 4 – 10 soldiers, Platoon 3 – 4 Squads or 16 – 40 men, Company 3 – 4 Platoons or 100 – 200 soldiers, Battalion 3 – 5 Companies or 500 – 600 soldiers, Brigade 3 or more Battalions with 3,000 – 5,000 soldiers.

"We only have 32 Rangers here now, not even a full Platoon, and we don't have the TALOS Warriors. The situation just became serious. Corporal Phillips told me about the coded message so it seems we do have a spy on Tocabaga. I think that's how FPF found out the trucks were leaving for SOCOM. We need to find this spy ASAP, however my first priority is finding my missing Rangers.

"I need your help since you know St. Petersburg better than my men do. I want you to do a recon of the Dome area and the Dali location. I selected you, Tommy, Sergeant Major Willis, and First Sergeant Hammer for this job. They're on the way here now so we can discuss the details."

Sessions no sooner finished speaking and in walked Willis stating, "Sergeant Major Willis and First Sergeant Hammer reporting as ordered Sir." Willis had just flown back to Fort Desoto after escorting Sergeant First Class Dale's body to SOCOM for proper burial.

Hammer is a big bruiser who was in great shape. He stood about 6 foot 5 inches tall with muscles popping out of his shirt. He's a good-looking man with short brown hair and a square shaped jaw. His nick name is SLEDGE HAMMER because he can beat any man in a fight with his two giant fists. This was the first time I had the pleasure of meeting him.

"At ease gentlemen and take a seat. As you know we're here to plan a recon of the Dome area and Dali location to find our missing Rangers. Jack and Tommy are familiar with downtown St. Petersburg so the patrol will be made up of you four men. We need to do this tonight so Tommy do you have any ideas how to proceed with this recon?"

Tommy answered, "We know there's a curfew downtown at 2200 hours. I suggest that we insert into the area at midnight. We leave here at 2330 hours. I'd like a Black Hawk to fly surveillance an hour before we leave. I suggest we have a Humvee drop us off on Route 275 at the 22nd Ave. South exit. That's far enough away so no one will spot us and it's close enough to save us some humping time.

"We know the Feds have check points on all the main streets going into the city, so we'll take the back streets and alleys. The Dome is about a two mile hike from our drop off point and the Dali is about three miles. I estimate it will take us about four hours to complete the mission. Have a truck pick us up at the insertion point at 0500 hours. If we're early we'll hump it down Route 275 back to Tocabaga.

The Feds (Federal Police Force) have security patrols roaming around at night as well as check points on the major streets in the Green Zone. The security guards keep criminals and gangs out but also keep the ordinary hard working people in line. In the old days before the Government takeover we would go downtown every weekend to the movies, so we're very familiar with the streets and buildings.

The so-called Green Zone or FPF Protected Zone runs North and South from 5th Street South to 5th Street North. East and West it runs from Interstate 275 to the shore line of Tampa Bay. It's in this area where the FPF has check points and roving patrols.

"For weapons I suggest we each carry a handgun with a silencer and night laser sights. We'll need M4 carbines with suppressors and 300 rounds. I think bringing a couple of grenades is also a good idea. Anyone else have any thoughts on weapons or gear?"

Willis commented, "For tactical gear we need night vision FLIRs and tactical radio headsets. I'll bring along radio headsets that have dual in-ear buds with digital hearing and combat noise suppression. These units only transmit a half mile so hopefully they can't be jammed."

FLIR (Forward Looking Infrared) are night vision goggles that use thermal imaging. They are capable of detecting very small differences in heat or thermal energy given off by any object thereby, turning night into day.

Hammer asked in a deep rough voice, "Should we wear standard camouflage?"

Tommy replied, "Wear standard night camouflage and paint your face and hands black. We need to blend into the shadows. Once we are on the move in the city we'll pair up. Since Jack and I know the area best I suggest Hammer and Jack stay together. Willis will be with me in case of a split up. If our radios aren't working due to jamming then meet back at the drop off point. If no one is there lay low until 0500 hours the pickup time."

Hammer advised, "I'll bring along a glass cutter, wire cutter, and a small pry bar."

I replied, "That's a good idea. We may need them."

We pulled a map up on the computer of downtown St. Petersburg and printed out a copy for everyone. I highlighted the route we would follow. One problem was some of the houses we would pass might still have people living in them. If we're spotted by anyone living in the Green Zone they will surely report us to the FPF.

As everyone was reading the map, I said, "From the insertion point we take 22nd Ave. east to 16th Street and go north directly to Tropicana Field. Once at the Dome we will need to climb or cut a 12 foot fence. Once past the fence we need to roam around the Dome looking for a window or door to enter.

"The hard part will be going to the Dali from the Dome. We'll go back the way we came on 16th Street to 7th Ave. and head east to 9th Street. We take 9th Street north to 6th Ave. which we follow all the way to the Airport perimeter fence. Then we move along the fence perimeter to the Dali. There may be a lot of security in this area but there are trees and buildings we can use for cover.

"To withdraw from the Dali we'll take 3rd

Street south all the way to 22nd Ave. and go west to Route 275. Anyone have a question." No one replied.

"Ok that sounds like a good plan. Willis you and Hammer pick up Jack and Tommy at 2230 hours sharp. Now let's discuss the spy, Jack," Sessions said.

"Well I have a list of possible people and one in particular. Guy Allen seems to be the most logical person but we have no actual proof. We need to hear the message to see if we can recognize the voice."

We all walked into the radio room and Phillips played the message. A recorded male voice said, "21 11 21 0 7 9 6 24 16 8 0 15 22 21 7 0 7 12 24 0 26 7 0 22 18 20 19 7 0 11 14 0 20 12 18 13 20 0 7 12 0 8 12 24 12 14 0 25 18 20 0 7 6 13 26."

"Does anyone recognize that voice?" I asked. No one replied. If there was any accent I couldn't detect one.

"I guess the male voice rules out Ellen being a spy," Tommy commented.

Sessions stated, "Well we didn't learn anything from listening to it so we need to decode the damn thing. I'll send it to SOCOM but I doubt they have time to break the code while they're under attack. Phillips, relay that message to Captain

Myers at SOCOM Intel. Tell him it's urgent he breaks the code because we have a spy on Tocabaga and our security is at risk."

I asked Phillips to provide me a copy of the coded message on a memory chip so I could play it back and listen to it again in my spare time.

Phillips went to relay the message and came back right away advising Sessions, "Captain, SOCOM didn't acknowledge receiving the message. I think the radio signal is being jammed."

Sessions responded, "Well that makes a lot sense because cutting enemy communications is the first thing we do when going into battle. Phillips, send the message by cable. They can't jam that. From now on use cable to communicate with SOCOM.

"What's your plan to find this spy Jack?"

"Tommy and Jim Bo were going to snoop around today and see if they can find a CB radio in GA's house, boat, or car. I believe he went fishing this morning so now is a perfect time to search his house and car. It's not legal but we have no choice."

"Jack, this is basically war and you can't follow the normal civilian laws all the time. We have a spy here and that means we have to take the gloves off and do whatever is necessary to find him."

"Thanks for that comment, Captain, and you're correct. Ron is going to follow GA around and see what he's doing. He'll also ask some of our most trusted people if they have seen anything suspicious.

"Everyone needs to be aware that Guy has three friends that came with him from Georgia. Dew, Barry, and Zack are close friends who live with GA."

I don't worry about Dew, Barry, or Zack because they weren't around when God passed out brains. They do whatever GA tells them to so I call them the three stooges. I don't think any of them can read or write let alone think on their own.

Captain Sessions asked, "Why don't we … the Rangers arrest him and his three buddies then we'll hold them until you obtain proof."

"It's not that easy because we also have four other suspects but GA is the primary one. We can't go around arresting people who haven't committed a crime. The citizens of Tocabaga wouldn't like that. It would create a lot of tension between us."

"Yes I agree. That's a good point. We don't want any hard feelings with our friends on

Tocabaga."

"If nothing else, Captain, let us get to work and find out who's the spy. I don't know if we can find out who it is before we do the recon tonight but we'll try our best."

Looking at my watch it was 0900 hours and I already had a headache from the meeting and needed a drink. Ron took up his post near the dock where GA would come back after fishing. After GA leaves his boat Ron would search it for a CB radio.

Tommy and Jim Bo hurried down to search his house and car. GA could be coming back at any time depending on how good the fishing was. I went home to replay the message a few more times in hopes I would hear something that I missed. I wanted to write the code down to see if I could break it.

It was 1300 hours when Tommy, Jim Bo, and Ron came to my house.

"Well did you find anything?" I asked.

"Negative. No radio," replied Tommy.

"I checked his boat which has a standard marine radio but no CB radio," Ron replied.

I told them, "I listened to the message at least twenty times but I still don't know who it is."

Just then little Johnny, my ten year-old

adopted grandson, ran into the room and asked, "Hey what are you guys doing?" I handed him the piece of paper with the code written on it and played the message for him to hear.

I told him, "That's a code and we are trying to find out what it means."

Johnny said, "My Dad did codes when he worked for the government. Sometimes I would help him write the codes. I know a lot about them. I think this is an alphabet number code or similar to a ROT 1 code. There're many types of codes; Morse, number, and transposition codes."

Johnny rescued Captain Sessions from al-Qaida and saved his little brother Jimmy from being killed. His full name is Johnny Evans. I never asked Johnny what his father did for a living. I never discussed it with him because his Mom and Dad were murdered by al-Qaida. I didn't want to bring up the past since Johnny and his brother had seen a lot of terrible things that little kids should never see. It seems that his Father was in the Military or did some kind of spy work for the DOD or DIA (Defense Intelligence Agency).

We all just sat there in amazement that little ten year old Johnny knew so much about codes. I knew he was smart but not this smart. I asked him, "Johnny can you tell us what it says?"

"Sure, Grandpa, give me some time. I'll be right back."

Johnny got up, leaving the room with the paper that had the code written on it and went to his bedroom. We ate lunch and had just finished when he came back declaring, "I think I got it. I am sure it's a number alphabet code. This was easy to break. You assign a number to each letter in the alphabet. In this case they just numbered it backwards. I think number 26 is letter A and number 25 is letter B and so forth. Spaces between words are a zero."

Johnny handed us the paper. Our mouths dropped as I read it out loud, "FPF TRUCKS LEFT TOC AT EIGHT PM GOING TO SOCOM BIG TUNA"

I replied, "Johnny, good job. You solved a big problem and for helping us I am going to teach you how to shoot. I know you want to learn so in a few days we'll go shooting."

"Great, Grandpa. That sounds awesome."

Johnny ran out of the room yelling, "Mom … Dad and Grandpa are going to teach me how to shoot a gun!"

Just then my granddaughters, Kendra and

Shanda, came in the room and they both said, "We want to learn how to shoot, Grandpa."

"Ok girls I'll think about it."

Tommy told me, "Now you did it. Everyone wants to learn how to shoot. They're too young."

I reminded Tommy, "You were 10 years old when I took you shooting for the first time." Tommy didn't say a word after I refreshed his memory.

"Ok we have to find out who's BIG TUNA. Let's go around and ask people we can trust if they ever heard of anyone called BIG TUNA."

I called Captain Sessions and told him that little Johnny broke the coded message and Sessions said, "That kid is very special. He's Army Ranger material." I read Sessions the message and advised him we don't know who the BIG TUNA is.

Then Kendra said, "We know where a Big Tuna is."

Shanda spoke up, "Yep we know a Big Tuna."

I asked, "Ok, who do you think is Big Tuna?"

Kendra replied, "It's not a person silly. It's a boat."

Shanda butted in, "Yep it's a big white fishing boat." That blew my mind; the kids knew more than I did. Leave it to the kids to figure things out.

"Ok, tell me where the boat is." They both giggled.

"It's at the High and Dry lot near the bridge. We saw it one day while walking with Mom," Kendra said.

"It's not in the water. It's an old boat sitting way in the back. It has the name Big Tuna on it," Shanda told me.

Kendra is my Son's daughter and she is 10 years old. Kendra is very active climbing trees and running all over the place. She's a real tomboy. Shanda is my adopted granddaughter. Actually my daughter Amy adopted her after her Mother was murdered by gang members. Shanda will never know this but her father was a bully and gang member that I killed in a gun fight. Shanda and Kendra play together all the time since they're the same age.

I told my spy hunters, "Let's go see the Big Tuna."

The girls asked, "Can we go too?"

"No I want you both to stay here because we don't know who owns that boat and there could be trouble. Thank you for your help girls, we'll be back soon."

We all jumped up and made a dash into the garage to obtain our guns from my Liberty safe. I have three big Liberty safes that I purchased years ago. One safe is for guns and two are used for ammunition. We always store our guns in the safe to keep them away from the kids. The kids have been schooled never to touch any gun otherwise they'd be in big trouble. I put the fear of God in them.

The four of us picked up our M4 carbines given to us by the Rangers and holstered our Glock 9 mm handguns. We put on our bullet proof vests and got into Jim's pickup truck. It's a short three minute drive to the High and Dry lot located near the main Tocabaga Bridge. As we pulled in the lot we could see the boat back in the corner near a fence.

A High and Dry is a storage building for boats so boats can be stored inside out of the weather. There is also a large lot where boats can be stored outside. This one has about ten boats stored outside and twenty inside.

We were a good 50 yards away and I told Jim, "Stop here. Let's sit here a minute to see if anyone is on the boat." We waited five minutes and didn't see anyone so we proceeded to the boat.

Pulling up next to it the first thing I saw was a radio antenna. We dismounted and I advised my crew, "You guys stay here and keep a look out. I'm going on the boat to see if there's a CB radio."

It was an old fishing boat about 35 feet long. I climbed over the transom and looked around in the cockpit. There was no radio so I decided to go into the cabin. The cabin door was locked so I kicked it open. Old clothes and papers were scattered all over the cabin. Searching through the junk I found a CB radio, covered with a cloth, sitting on a shelf next to the sink. Yes, it was a CB radio all right. I turned it on … it worked and it was tuned to channel 19. I took a bandana out of my pocket, unplugged the radio, and carefully wrapped it up to preserve any fingerprints.

Leaving the cabin I told my men, "I found a CB radio and it was hooked up. Tommy, take this and put it in the truck. Be careful not to touch it because I want Sessions to check it for fingerprints." I handed the radio down to him over the transom where the words BIG TUNA were painted.

Ron asked me, "Who owns this boat anyway?"

"I have no idea who owns it but the main point is who owns this CB radio. Let's get out of here before someone sees us."

Just as we were leaving GA and his men were driving right towards us in his old white pickup truck. They had spotted us so we all racked our guns and I told my group, "Take it easy and act friendly. Don't let on that we think they're spies."

GA pulled up next to us and asked, "Hey. Y'all lost over here? What are you doing here?" His friends were glaring at us. I could sense they had their handguns at the ready.

I replied, "Hi GA how you doing? We're just looking around checking things out. How about you guys, what y'all doing?"

"Not much, just out here trying to fix a boat motor."

"Ok we gotta go, see ya later." As we pulled out of the lot GA sat there watching us. He had no clue that we knew he was a spy.

I told Jim Bo, "Park by the bridge and we'll watch them. Pretend to be doing something, maybe check your oil. I'm calling Sessions to send over backup."

Ron, Tommy, and I walked up the bridge while glancing around to see what GA was doing. GA drove towards the boat. He got out of the truck and climbed into the boat. I told my family to get ready for trouble.

I called Sessions telling him we found the CB radio and Big Tuna. We knew the spy was GA along with his three buddies because they just climbed into the BIG TUNA. I asked him to send a couple of Rangers to help arrest them. Sessions advised me Willis and Hammer will be there ASAP.

I had just hung up and looked up to see what GA was doing but it was too late. GA and his men were speeding towards us in his truck. He slammed on the brakes skidding to a stop next to Jim Bo as Tommy, Ron, and I ran down from the bridge to meet them with our guns at the ready.

GA and his men jumped out of their truck. GA yelled in Jim Bo's face, "Did you guys take my radio? If so hand it over now!" The fool just admitted it's his CB radio. That admission and the boat named BIG TUNA was proof enough they were the spies.

Approaching them I replied, "What radio you talking about?" I had my M4 pointed towards him but the barrel pointed down, aiming more at the ground, in a low ready position. His men had their hands on their pistols as if getting ready to draw.

"I had a CB radio on the boat and now it's gone."

I flicked off the safety putting my finger on the M4 trigger and was ready to rock and roll.

"Jack, I'm warning you don't point that gun at me!" Ron and Tommy were flanking his men and had their M4s in the low ready position.

"I'm not pointing my gun directly at you."

"I'm not going to tell you again sling your M4 or there is going to be trouble!" I watched GA put his hand on the grip of his Colt 45 Commander. If he started to draw I would kill him on the spot.

Looking out of the corner of my eye, I saw that Ron and Tommy were covering the other three men in low ready position. Jim Bo was standing there but his carbine was in the truck and his Glock was in its holster.

We were standing about 15 feet apart and I had enough of the bull shit. I told GA, "Ok cut the crap. We know you're a spy and we have your radio to prove it! Raise your hands! You're all under arrest!" Now my M4 was pointed directly at him.

"What are you going to do Jack shoot us in

cold blood?" Guy still had his hand on his gun.

"Raise your hands GA. Don't make me shoot you." GA started to draw his gun and so did his men.

At fifteen feet away I opened fire with 3 quick shots ... Bam ... Bam ... Bam. Ron and Tommy fired at all most the same time. I saw all four spies fall to the ground. Never, ever try to beat a rifle to the draw especially when the barrel is pointed directly at you. Guy's gun cleared the holster and as he was going down he managed to fire one shot.

Three bullets hit him in the chest knocking him down, but he was still alive. I walked up to him and took the gun out of his hand. He uttered, "This isn't over ... Jack," as blood flowed out of his mouth he went limp with his last breath.

Those were the last words out of his big mouth. One more dead Commie didn't bother me. Tommy and Ron had shot his three buddies peppering them full of holes. Tommy called out, "Zack and Barry are still alive, but Drew is dead."

I walked over to Zack and kicked his gun away. He only had one bullet wound in his left upper torso below the collar bone. He was very lucky to be alive. I bent down and asked him, "Who else is a spy?"

"Fuck you asshole," he replied.

I didn't like that smart answer so I took the end of my rifle barrel and shoved it into the bullet hole in his shoulder, blood squirted out, which caused him to scream out in pain. I asked him again while keeping pressure on his wound, "Who else is a spy?"

"Eat shit and die Jack."

"No Zack you eat shit and die." I accidently pulled the trigger; at least I thought it was an accident. I think he flinched and made me pull the trigger. The poor fool died on the spot.

Tommy was pointing his gun at Barry. I saw Barry was bleeding a lot. He had three critical bullet wounds, one in the leg, and two in the gut. Barry winced in pain and blurted out, "I'll tell you who's a spy. Just don't let me die. Please … don't kill me."

"Ok Barry who else is a spy?"

Barry softly breathed out, "Jo …," as he coughed up blood. That was the end for Barry. Damn it I didn't get a full name out of him. It sounded like he said Joe, John, or Johnny but I wasn't sure what he said.

I told Tommy, "Dispose of the bodies."

Tommy asked me, "Do you think Barry was

saying Johnny?"

"I don't know for sure but it does mean we have more spies. We killed the main trouble-makers so maybe the rest of them will fall in line now that the leaders are fish food."

I turned around and saw Jim Bo was down so I ran over to him. He was holding his arm in pain and he commented, "I'm hit."

I could see the blood so I pulled out my Black Bear knife and cut his sleeve open. A 45 caliber bullet makes a nasty big ass hole in your body. He was bleeding but he was lucky as it appeared the bullet didn't hit anything major. It was an ugly looking flesh wound to his shoulder. Ron came over and tied a cloth around the wound putting pressure on it to help stop the bleeding.

Willis and Hammer finally arrived and saw the four dead bodies. Willis commented, "I guess we're a little too late. Did you have to kill them, Jack?"

"They drew down on us. You gotta be a stupid fool to draw down on someone with a carbine aimed at you. I'll write a report to Sessions telling him what happened. Right now I have to take Jim Bo to the clinic and I need some rest before our recon tonight."

Our security guards walked down from the

bridge and asked what was going on? Tommy filled them in on details that Guy and his friends where spies for the FPF. Everyone was surprised to hear we had spies on Tocabaga. They pitched in and helped Tommy drag the bodies over to the seawall. After throwing them into the dark blue water it didn't take long for the sharks to start feeding. We don't give funerals to traitors and scum bags.

I drove Jim Bo to the Clinic where Doc. Scott patched him up. He lost a piece of meat about the size of a silver dollar off his shoulder but otherwise he'll be fine in a few weeks. Doc gave Jim some antibiotics and pain killers for later. We went to the bar next door and had a couple shots of Jim Beam. After that we headed home for some much needed rest and food.

Tommy woke me up at 2200 hours for the recon patrol. I could barely move my old bones out of bed. I told my wife earlier I was going on a sneak and peek along with Tommy looking for the Rangers who were MIA. Needless to say she wasn't happy about it.

I needed a smoke and a strong cup of java to wake up. I was taking my first sip of coffee when Sessions phoned me and advised, "The Black Hawk recon flight showed nothing unusual at the Dome or Dali areas. Good luck tonight."

"Thanks Captain, I just hope we find your

missing men."

Tommy and I checked our gear making sure everything was secure and nothing would rattle or make noise while we were stalking around. We waited outside for Willis and Hammer while having a smoke. They pulled up and without saying a word to each other we rolled out of Tocabaga exactly at 2330 hours.

GA and his dirt balls were trying to cause an insurrection or rebellion. They were working with the FPF who wanted to take over Tocabaga. I wondered who else on Tocabaga is a spy. I'll really have to watch my back from now on because this thing is far from over.

JUNE 28, 2025

We drove to the insertion point in two Humvees. It was midnight when we dismounted from the trucks and watched them drive away as we hid on the side of the road in high weeds. There was a half moon shining which seemed to light up the dark night. We scanned the area for people or vehicles and found it was all clear.

Years ago, before the collapse, Route 275 was a busy highway. Now in the day time a car or two will roll down 275 carrying desperate people. People are trying to escape the madness and dangers of the city. If you are lucky enough to have a car it won't get you far because there's a gas shortage. At night there is no traffic because everyone is afraid of gang attacks. Make no mistake, if you run into a gang they'll kill you and your family, stealing everything from your dead bodies for the fun of it.

We took a minute to put on our tactical radio headsets and test them out. Using these we could whisper to each other and no one else could hear us unless they were standing right next to you.

The team moved single file down the 22nd Ave. entrance ramp with Tommy in the lead followed by Willis, then Hammer, and I was last in line. We moved along stealth like, slightly bent over, keeping low next to the guard rail to provide cover. Lucky for us the street lights weren't working due to power shortages. We stopped and scanned the area for a few minutes before proceeding down into the danger zone, which was 22nd Avenue.

Our team headed east along 22nd Ave. for about six blocks until we reached 16th Street south. Then we turned north on 16th Street which would take us straight to the Dome. There're many homes along this street so we needed to be alert. Some homes have people living in them and some are vacant. It's dark and since there aren't any street lights or house lights you can't tell which house is occupied. Some of these people own guns and have guard dogs. The FPF doesn't patrol here at night. They won't risk going outside of their patrol zones for fear of being attacked.

We proceeded down 16th Street stopping at each house looking and listening for any people. We proceeded one at a time moving slowly past each home as we headed toward the Dome.

We had to be vigilant while walking not to accidently kick a bottle or can thereby making unnecessary noise. There was a lot of junk and rubble on the ground. It looked like a war zone as many homes had been vandalized and stripped of their contents. Most had broken windows and doors. We saw chairs, broken tables, and even a toilet lying in the street. The city hasn't picked up the garbage in years. I thought how lucky we are to live on Tocabaga.

It's very stressful to walk along and look thru the night vision goggles. We took them off because the light from the half moon was sufficient. We can't risk letting anyone see us, so anyone who spots us will have to be eliminated. A handgun with a silencer is best to use for close range termination since it only makes a slight popping noise like pricking a balloon filled with air.

As we were sneaking along 16th Street Tommy stopped and I heard his voice whisper over the radio, "Three people at 2 o'clock, and a dog about 100 feet away on the porch." We all froze in our tracks and slumped down into the shadows of the bushes making us invisible.

The dog stood up and looked in our direction. It jumped off the porch and started coming towards us. It looked like an old mutt of some kind. As the dog came closer I saw its tail wagging. It didn't bark as it walked up to Tommy. Tommy stuck out his hand for the dog to smell him. He pulled a snack of some kind from his pocket and gave it to the dog. Thank God this was someone's friendly family pet and not a guard dog.

All of a sudden one of the men stood up and yelled, "Rex, get back here!" He yelled again and came down the porch steps with what looked like a shotgun in his hands. The other two men just sat there talking. The guy was coming across the street in our direction and he yelled again for the dog. The old dog suddenly turned around and ran to his master. He patted the dog on the head while saying good boy and headed back to the porch not knowing how close he came to death.

Tommy said over the radio, "That was close. Follow me we're going to avoid this house by going thru the back yard." We didn't like going through the back yards because of the junk laying around and sometimes there were high fences which greatly impeded our progress.

Following Tommy we went around to the back of the house passing through the back yard. I looked at my watch and saw it was now 0100 hours. It took us an hour to cover ten blocks. We were at 12th Ave. and had seven more blocks to reach the Dome. We needed to speed up our recon to complete the mission on time.

Finally we reached Interstate 175 and we could see the Dome on the other side of the six lane highway. Interstate 175 is really the exit and entrance route to downtown St. Petersburg. It's only about 1.5 miles long and runs in an east/west direction or in and out of downtown.

Laying in the weeds behind a small concrete berm we scanned the road and spotted four security trucks parked in the middle of the highway about half a mile away. The FPF men were standing next to their trucks talking. Unless they moved we would have to go further west which would waste more time. After waiting 15 minutes they finally drove off east toward downtown.

Tommy was the first to run across the six lane interstate. He made it across in lighting speed and he radioed for us to cross over. After crossing the highway we jumped over a three foot high concrete barrier landing in high grass. Keeping low we peered into the darkness looking for any security patrols. Next we had to cross a small side road and cut an entrance hole in a chain link fence to enter the Dome parking lot. Once we reached the fence there wasn't any cover except for the high grass and weeds.

We huddled up to discuss the situation and Tommy said, "One of us needs to cut a hole in the fence while we cover him. Once the hole is cut we'll run across the parking lot to the Dome and blend in with the shadows along the building."

Hammer volunteered, "Give me the cutters. I can cut the fence faster than any of you."

We all agreed since Hammer was strong he could use the wire cutters with ease. We watched him lope to the fence and start to cut the hole. Just then a security truck slowly came around the building moving counter clockwise shining a spot light. Hammer hit the ground and laid flat as he could. The search light passed right over him and the truck moved on going out of sight around the building.

Hammer finished cutting the hole and we saw him sprint to the Dome. We all followed in double time manner. As we huddled together up against the Dome,   Tommy whispered, "Let's proceed clockwise around the building since the security truck was moving counter-clockwise. That way if it comes back we'll spot it right away. Jack since you are last in line keep a heads up just in case the truck comes from behind us.

"We need to find a window or door. I prefer a window to crawl in because doors could be guarded or have an alarm. Let's move it."

We all agreed and moved out keeping about ten feet apart within a few feet of the Dome wall. After about 10 minutes we finally found a window. The window was up high and the only one that could reach it was Hammer. Hammer stood on his toes and peeked inside advising it was all clear. He tried to open it but it was locked so he took out the glass cutter, stuck a suction cup on the glass, and cut the pane. When the glass was cut he tapped it three or four times and pulled on the cup. The glass pane popped out clean as a whistle. Hammer reached in unlocked the window and pushed it open saying, "Welcome to the Dome."

Tommy whispered, "Hammer give Willis and me a boost up. You both stay here and wait for us."

Hammer boosted Tommy up to the window. He grabbed the ledge and climbed inside the building. He advised it was all clear for Willis to enter. Next Hammer boosted Willis up and he slid inside.

Hammer and I hid in the shadows waiting for their return. I heard a vehicle coming and warned Hammer. We ducked down low in a dark corner as the security truck went by us shining their spot light above our heads. It seemed the truck was patrolling around the Dome every 30 minutes. Tommy was right the truck went counter-clockwise around the Dome. I looked at my watch; it was now 0215 hours.

Hammer and I sat in the shadows for about 40 minutes and then we heard two men talking. We saw two security guards approaching on foot patrolling around the perimeter. They were coming our way shining a bright flashlight around the building. I told Hammer, "Lay flat as you can." We both pulled out our handguns. They were getting closer and closer to us with each step.

They stopped twenty feet away directly in front of us and one guy said, "Look. That window is broken. It wasn't broken an hour ago." Looking up he walked over to the window and didn't see us laying on the ground a few feet away in the darkness.

He said to his buddy, "I can't reach the window from out here. We'll have to check it from inside." That was my clue we needed to kill these two guards because if they're going inside they might run into Tommy and Willis. I couldn't see what Hammer was doing and we couldn't speak to each other so I aimed my gun at the guard's head as he walked away and fired two shots ... POP ... POP ... and then I heard a ... POP ... from Hammer's gun. Both guards slumped to the ground. I stood up, walked over to them, and shot each man in the head one more time. We dragged the bodies to a nearby dumpster and threw them inside.

The radio hissed and Tommy's voice came on, "We found four Rangers and Carl Jr. locked in a cell. There're about 200 other people locked up in here. We also saw the semi trucks. There are ten guards inside here, but we didn't see any BOTs. We're coming out now so be at the window."

I replied, "Roger. All clear out here." Hammer heard the conversation and we moved back to wait at the window. Three minutes later Tommy and Willis crawled out the window and silently dropped to the ground.

I told Tommy and Willis, "We had to kill two guards because they saw the broken window pane. They were going to go inside and check it out so we had to pop them. Did you get some pictures of the lay out to show Sessions?"

"Yep we got it all on video and still pics. I think we should rescue these guys and take them back with us now," Willis told us.

"That's not our mission Willis. We have to recon the Dali to see if they are still making BOTs,"

I commented back.

All three agreed with me because we didn't have any wheels to make a quick escape. There's no telling how many Federal Police would come after us.

Continuing on with our mission we crossed back over 175 and headed down 16th Street toward 7th Ave. South. We were disappointed to leave the Rangers there but we had no choice. Orders are orders and they must be followed.

We reached 6th Ave. with no problems. We didn't encounter a single person. The good thing about 6th Ave. is there are no houses on this street, only old office and business buildings. However, there could still be people living in this area. The satellite map showed us there're many trees and bushes that can be used for cover as well as alleys to hide in.

Proceeding down 6th Ave. we reached two large buildings around 5th Street. A considerable number of people were standing outside drinking and smoking pot. We needed to bypass them so we headed around to the back of building to cut through the alley way. Passing along the back of the building it was very dark because the buildings blocked the moon light, making black shadows.

Behind office buildings, in the alley ways, is where all the trash is kept in big dumpsters. Long ago garbage trucks would come once a week and empty the dumpster and take the trash to be burned or put in a land fill. Many bums or homeless people would hang out in the alleys to pick up any food that may have been thrown away. We called it dumpster diving because you literally had to dive into the big metal container.

As we passed by one dumpster I heard a noise from inside. The lid was open so I peeked over the top and looked while holding my Glock. I thought maybe there's a rat or raccoon inside. As I peered over the edge with my night vision goggles on they saw me and huddled together in fear. I must have been a scary looking sight with my face painted black looking like I had on war paint.

"Please don't hurt us, Mister," one said in a high female voice. Three kids were sitting on a pile of rotten garbage that made me gag from the stench. In their hands they had some kind of rancid looking food.

I took off my goggles and moved closer advising them, "Don't worry kids I'm here to help you." I held out my hand and waved my fingers for them to come over to me.

"Come on kids we're not going to hurt you. We're here to help you. I have some food for you." I pulled three power bars out of my pocket and held them up.

Now the rest of my crew came over and looked in the container. Willis asked, "Now what are we going to do?"

I told Willis, "We're going to help them."

The three kids hesitantly climbed out and I handed them each a power bar which they ripped open and gobbled up in a few bites. I asked them, "Where are your parents?"

The girl replied, "Our parents are dead. We lived in the Green Zone and there wasn't enough food. They were killed by the Federal Police for stealing food. The Police shot them and made us leave the Green Zone."

"How long ago was that?"

Looking at them you could tell these kids have had a tough time. Their clothes were filthy and so were their bodies. As a matter of fact they smelled like garbage. The girl's hair was matted and falling out probably due to malnutrition. She was a skinny-looking thing and her hands were shaking from the lack of food. Her face was sunken in and I thought she could be close to death. The two boys didn't look any better. I gave them each another power bar which they quickly devoured.

The girl said, "I think about a year ago our parents were killed. I've been trying to take care of my brothers but there isn't enough food here. We don't have any other place to go. Who are you guys?"

"We're with the Army Rangers. What are your names and how old are you?"

"I'm 15 and my name is Rosie. Billy is 13 and Peter is 9 years old."

Billy said, "Would you Army guys please take my sister with you 'cause the men around here make her trade sex for food? One man hurt her so I hit him in the head with a pipe. If he touches her again I'll kill him. My brother and I can make it ok. I just want my sister to be safe."

"Billy you look pretty beat up. How did you get those black eyes?"

"The guy I hit with the pipe had his friends beat me."

"Where are they now Billy?"

"Oh they're around somewhere. They're tough mean guys and they run this part of town."

"Don't worry about them Billy, you're all going to be safe now. You can come with us to Tocabaga."

"I've of heard of Tocabaga but I didn't think it was real. Isn't that an island where people live and have food to eat every day?"

"That's right. We're all going there tonight."

"That sounds great. Do you think I can become an Army Ranger and fight the bad guys?"

"Probably, when you're old enough."

I told my recon team, "We can't leave these kids here alone they're going to die for sure. I suggest you three complete the mission and I'll take them to the extraction point and wait for you there."

Hammer replied, "I don't like it but they're kids that need help so I agree."

Tommy and Willis concurred so I told the kids, "Ok we have to walk about three miles to our truck. Kids you stay close to me and do what I do. If I stop then you stop, if I hide then you hide. You guys got it?"

"Yes sir, Mister," said Rosie.

"My name is Gunn, Jack Gunn. You can just call me Jack."

Billy said, "Yes sir, Mister Jack."

We headed out toward 3rd Street where we would part ways with the recon team. They would continue straight to the airport. We would turn south on 3rd St. and go to 22nd Ave. heading east to the extraction point at Interstate 275.

Upon reaching 3rd Street I wished my recon team good luck and we parted ways. As we were walking along I noticed that Peter was limping and dropping behind. He couldn't keep up so I asked him, "Peter, what's wrong with your foot?"

"I cut my toe real bad on some glass and it hurts a lot."

"Let me see it." We stopped behind some bushes next to an old building. Peter sat down and took off his worn out tattered shoe. He didn't have any socks on his feet; none of them wore any socks. He held his dirty foot up and I shined my flashlight on it. It was a badly infected cut with puss running out of it. I washed it off with water and put some antibiotic cream on the wound. Peter winced in pain as I wrapped a bandage around it and helped him put his shoe back on.

"Jump on my back I'll carry you for a while to give our foot a rest.

"Billy can you carry my backpack for me?"

"You bet I can, Mr. Jack." I took it off and handed the 30 pound pack to him. I kneeled down and Peter wrapped his arms around my neck then put his feet around my waist. I guessed that Peter was only about 35 pounds. A kid his age should be at least 60 pounds, but he was just skin and bones.

"Peter, when we get back to Tocabaga we'll have the Doctor look at that cut. Ok kids let's get going. We still have a long hike ahead of us." I didn't want to tell Peter but I think gangrene had set in and he could lose his toe or maybe his foot. He could lose his life if it wasn't treated soon.

I could tell these kids were polite, kind children. They helped each other stay alive in the concrete jungle for a year and that's not easy to do. I can only imagine what Rosie had to endure. It made me want to kill every dirtbag that ever touched her.

We had no sooner stepped out from behind the bushes with Peter on my back and standing in our way were four men with handguns. They were about fifty feet away from us and one of them yelled, "Hey! What y'all doing with my kids?"

Billy whispered, "That's them, they're the ones that hurt my sister and beat me."

I put Peter down and told the kids to get behind the bushes. I flipped my safety off and put the M4 on full automatic. I yelled back to them, "Oh these are your kids. Sorry, I just wanted to have some fun you know what I mean."

Another jerk asked me, "You're all dressed up like an Army guy. Who do you think you are …

GI Joe?" They all laughed.

I was out-numbered but not out-gunned. I looked at their handguns to determine the caliber. I couldn't tell in the dark but they looked like small caliber guns. I figured my bullet proof vest would stop those rounds if I got shot.

The same guy yelled, "Hey Rosie, you little whore, get out here where I can see you." Of course Rosie didn't come out in the open.

The four men were starting to spread out to create space between them and were moving closer to me. As they were moving closer I thought now is the time to take them out.

The same asshole yelled to me, "Mister, hand over your gun. You're no match for the four of us. We've killed a few guys like you before. Give us your gun and we'll let you go!"

"You mean this gun," as I pointed it at them and pulled the trigger firing on full auto, creating a spray pattern of deadly bullets. I dropped down to one knee to reduce my target size and kept firing taking careful aim at each man.

I heard one or two of their guns fire and saw flashes but they missed me. Three scum bags fell to the ground but the fourth dork was running for cover across the street. I slowly took aim putting my laser on him and squeezed the trigger … BAM …

my bullet hit his head exploding it like a ripe watermelon.

I knew he was dead so I got up and walked over to the three jerks laying on the ground. Two were dead but one was still alive and cried, "Please don't kill me, Mister!" I kicked the gun away from his hand.

The three kids walked up next to me and Billy pointed at the man saying, "He's the guy. He's the one that hurt Rosie."

This jerk looked like a real piece of shit. He had long matted hair and of course a beard that was gray in color. He was kind of scary looking with his long witch-like nose and beady eyes. His face was almost black from all the dirt on it. I wanted to blow his head off and kill him on the spot.

I told the dork, "I'm not going to kill you. I'm going to hurt you real bad then God is going to kill you for what you did to these kids."

I looked at the dork and he had at least 2 wounds in his upper torso. He was as good as dead so I thought I might as well help him suffer a little more. I fired the M4 shooting four rounds into his leg. With each shot his body jumped in the air and he screamed in pain. Then I pointed the M4 barrel at his crotch, pressed the barrel on it, and fired one more round. That really made him jump and scream. That was the least I could do for a bully and child molester. They should all be shot on sight.

We stood there a few minutes watching the life drain from his body and the worm finally died. The kids didn't say one word as I walked around picking up the handguns and tossed them down the sewer drain in the street. I commented, "Well they won't be hurting any more kids. They're going to hell."

I picked up Peter and as we started walking again Billy told me, "I want to be a Ranger like you, Mister Jack."

"Billy I'm not a Ranger. Rangers are better warriors than I am. They are better trained and younger than me. I have a lot of experience and training but I am not an Army Ranger. Do you know what the Ranger motto is Billy?"

"No. What's their motto?"

"Rangers Lead the Way."

"What does that mean?"

"It means just what it says. The Rangers are always leading the way into battle. They are the first ones to be called on because they are the best the Army has. Not everyone can become a Ranger. You have to pass a lot of tests before you are accepted. I think you could become a Ranger some day if you really want to."

"Mister Jack, can you teach me about guns and how to shoot?"

"Yep I'll teach you how to shoot. That's one thing I am good at." We continued walking without any further chatter.

It took us 30 minutes to reach 22nd Ave. where we stopped to rest. At the corner of 3rd and 22nd there is an old house that was owned by my father. It was boarded up and vacant now. We went into the back yard so no one could see us. Putting Peter down I reached up above the door frame and found the key that was hidden there years ago. I went in the house to check if it was safe. The old house had no furniture ever since my father passed on years ago. I looked in each room and it was all clear. I waved the kids to come inside and we flopped down on the floor exhausted.

In the old days this was a safe place to live. I recall all the neighbors coming over on Thanksgiving Day for turkey and steaks which my brother Ron would donate free of charge. It was a mixed neighborhood where your skin color or religion didn't matter because everyone was friends. In those days neighbors helped each other.

This area is now a dangerous gang-infested zone all the way to 34th Street. The gangs roam at night doing their dirty deeds, getting high on pot, crack, or meth. They are dangerous and would kill me, take my guns, and kidnap the children. The kids would be used as sex slaves or sold.

Rosie asked, "Whose house is this?"

"It belongs to my family now. My Mom and Dad use to live here years ago."

"You got a Mom and Dad?"

"No, not anymore, Rosie. They passed on a long time ago."

I gave the kids some water from my camelback and another power energy bar. I asked Peter, "How is your foot doing?"

"It feels pretty good."

"Do you think you can walk for a while?" Peter would have to walk now because I needed to have my hands free to use my weapons.

"Yeah, I can walk."

I looked at my watch and it was 0345 hours. I said, "We'll rest another 15 minutes and then leave." That would give us one hour to reach the extraction point.

Billy asked me, "How much further do we

have to go?" I heard voices from outside.

"Everyone be quite. Someone is outside. Follow me."

My Father had a safe room built years ago. There was a fire place and next to it was a hidden door built into the wall. The door looked like it was part of the wall. It was made from 6 inch thick hard wood and was lined with steel sheet metal. It could be locked from the inside and there were no windows or other doors into the room. It was pretty much bullet proof. The door opened out so it was impossible to bash in. The only problem was you couldn't see or shoot out because it had no viewing ports.

I took the kids into the hidden safe room and locked the door behind me. The safe room was "L" shaped so you could also hide behind a wall.

I heard one man yell, "Hey man this back door is open!" I heard them walk inside. There was no telling how many men were outside but I think I heard six different voices.

One gang member said, "This is cool man. How come we never been here before?"

Another one said, "What we gonna do

now?"

A reply came, "I don't know about y'all but I'm smoking a bud. After this smoke we gots to find some food and money. We gots to rob someone tonight."

Just then Billy sneezed and one gangster said, "Y'all hear? That someone's here."

Another replied, "I didn't hear shit. Hey Bro, y'all hearing stuff from being on that crack."

"I'm telling y'all I heard a sneeze from dat wall."

I could hear them walking on the tile floor and then they were knocking on the wall ... thump ... thump ... and then ... thud ... thud ... as they knocked on the hidden wooden door. You could tell a difference in the tone.

"I told y'all, why dat wall sound different here. Somethin' behind here for sure. I'm gonna kick it down."

I heard him kick the thick wooden door which he thought was a wall. He said, "Dam dat thing solid. Look around for a hammer or somethin'."

"Ain't no hammer in here. Shoot it, fool." I heard him rack a round. I could tell by the sound it was an AK47 so I told the kids to move behind the

57

wall with me.

He started to fire on full automatic and after firing 15 rounds he stopped. No bullets made it thru the door. He said, "We need to blow it up. Give me that RPG."

One smart jerk replied, "Fool y'all can't fire dat, it'll burn down the house." I hoped he wouldn't use the RPG because that will blow the door down and half the house. I was thinking of opening the door and shooting it out with them. I had the element of surprise on my side.

If I unlock the door and kick it open maybe it would hit one or two men knocking them down or off balance; then I could just lean out and shoot anyone I saw. If I did that I'd have to kill them all before they could use the RPG. Once I open the door I would have to finish the fight. Thinking further I realized it was too risky to try with the kids here.

I looked at my watch and it was 0410 hours. My team would be coming by here at any time. I can reach them on the radio if they are close by. I pushed the talk button and said, "Recon team reply, Recon team reply … need help …reply." I repeated my radio message every few minutes.

The gangsters were now bashing on the door with some type of heavy object. The door was shaking but held firm. After a few more blows I heard something start to crack. I was running out of time.

"Recon team, Jack here, reply." No reply was heard.

Then it occurred to me I had two hand grenades. All I needed to do was open the door a little and toss one out into the room. That would kill most of them. When they stop banging on the door I'll toss it out.

I advised the kids my plan and told them to cover their ears and stay behind the wall. I told them don't come out of the room until I tell you it's ok.

The jerks got tired and the banging stopped. One of them said, "That's hard work," as they walked away. I went to the door with the grenade in my right hand. I unlocked the door and opened it just enough to toss out the bomb. Pulling the pin I tossed it out into the middle of the room and quickly closed the door.

I heard one of them yell, "Shit, grenade!"

The M67 hand grenade is a small bomb that can be thrown by hand. It's designed to detonate after a set amount of time, usually about 4 seconds.

The M 67 is an anti-personnel fragmentation grenade that disperses lethal fragments upon detonation. If you're within a few meters then kiss your ass good-bye.

As soon as I closed the door … KABOOM … the grenade went off. I reached for my M4 and bolted out the door firing on full automatic. I sprayed the room with a full magazine of bullets and then jumped behind the big open wooden door for cover. I dropped the empty mag. and reloaded a new one. I popped my head out a little to see if anyone was still alive and saw five bodies on the floor.

BAAAAAAAAAM … A shower of bullets hit the door. I ducked and thought it came from the kitchen about 20 feet away. There're two ways into the kitchen one is through the family room, which I was in, and the other through the dining room. The family room is also connected to the dining room with a big-door way. He was in the kitchen hiding behind the wall. I decided to throw my last grenade right at the kitchen door. When it blows I'll run into the dining room. I hoped when he saw the grenade he'd run out the other kitchen door into the dining room, trying to escape the explosion, and then I'll have him in my sights. If he doesn't run, the grenade will kill him.

I pulled the pin and lobbed it to the kitchen door. KABOOM ... I dashed though a haze of smoke to the dining room and there he was standing right in front of me about 15 feet away.

Our eyes locked on each other as we both aimed and pulled our triggers at the same time. His trigger just went click, proving he was out of ammo, and I fired a burst into his chest until my ammo ran out. The impact of the bullets pushed him back to the wall. He fell dead as a door nail on the floor full of oozing bloody bullet holes.

I heard another man moaning so I drew my pistol and quickly moved around the room shooting all the jerks in the head to make sure they didn't come back to life like a zombie. I searched the bedrooms to see if anyone else was hiding in the house. Just then I heard on the radio, "Hey Jack, you in the house?" It was Tommy.

I turned around and standing in the doorway was my recon team. I said, "Hey you guys missed all the action. I could have used your help." My hands were trembling as I leaned up against the wall and lit up a smoke. I was very lucky the dirtbag ran out of ammo because his AK47 rounds would have penetrated my bullet proof vest.

"It looks like you didn't need any help. All we needed to do was follow the dead bodies to find you. I assume you killed the four men about six blocks from here," Willis commented.

"I had a run in with the men who hurt these kids so of course I had to kill them. We stopped to rest here and this doper gang shows up."

"Shit, Jack, you killed ten bad guys on this mission."

"How many have you guys killed?"

Willis answered, "I didn't know we were keeping count."

"I always keep count. The less dirtbags on this earth the better."

"Ok, you win Jack, but you have to admit it you attract bad guys like a magnet." Everyone laughed but me.

I yelled, "Kids, it's ok come on out!" Looking at my watch it was 0430 hours so we needed to move out double time. I just hoped we wouldn't run into anymore gangs.

I didn't like leaving the dead bodies in our house so we dragged them outside into the yard. Maybe the rats, dogs, or coyotes will eat them. As we left I locked the door and promised myself I'd be back to clean up the mess. I hid the RPG in the safe room because it may come in handy some day.

Tommy took the lead and I was last in line with the kids. This time Tommy took one side of the street and Willis the other to provide a cross fire if necessary. We were moving at a double time pace and Peter couldn't keep up so Hammer picked him up like a sack of rice putting him over his shoulder. I grabbed Rosie by the hand pulling her along forcing her keep up. Billy managed to stick with us.

If we saw anyone we would shoot and scoot. That means don't stop, just shoot and keep on moving. I heard Willis and Tommy fire at someone but I didn't see where the bullets went. No one was firing at us as we trotted down the street. We were almost at the extraction point when I looked behind me.

Coming up fast from behind was a crowd of people. They were running down the middle of the street after us so I yelled, "We got company behind us!" Hammer, Billy, and, with Rosie in tow, started running as fast as we could.

Willis and Tommy stopped as we ran by them. I watched them kneel down and fire on full auto into the crowd of people about 300 feet away. As bodies dropped to the street the crowd scattered. After the crowd dispersed, Willis and Tommy caught up to us as we were climbing the exit ramp to our extraction point on Interstate 275.

The Humvees were sitting there waiting for us. It was a great sight and a feeling of relief came over me. We jumped into the Hummers and took off as we heard bullets pinging off the back of the truck.

No one said a word as we sped away because we were too exhausted to speak. I was just starting to gain my breath back when I looked at Hammer and little Peter was curled up in his arms fast asleep. I glanced at the other kids; they were also asleep as we rumbled down the highway back to the safety of Tocabaga. I started to doze off and I heard Hammer say to me, "Jack you did a good deed saving these kids. You're a good guy in my book."

"You too, Hammer," as I sat there with my eyes closed. I thought to myself, *Thank you God, for giving me the strength to save these kids.*

We arrived safely back on Tocabaga at 0545 hours. The driver stopped at my house and I said, "Wake up kids. We're home now. Welcome to Tocabaga." Rubbing their eyes all three climbed out of the vehicle and looked around.

Hammer commented, "I'll stop by and check on the kids sometime today. See you later Peter." Hammer patted Peter on the head. I could tell Peter had just made a new friend. Willis just waved good-bye, he was probably too tired to talk, as they took off for the Fort.

My whole family was up waiting for us as

we walked in the door. Tommy and I were greeted with big hugs from all. The table was set with fried fish, hard boiled eggs, and fruit.

The kids I rescued stood there watching and I introduced them to my family. I told everyone, "I want you to meet Rosie, Billy, and Peter. They're part of our family now. Their Mother and Father were killed by the FPF and I found them downtown outside the Green Zone. They have no place to live so I brought them here."

Hemmi told them, "Kids come here, sit down, and have something to eat." They didn't need to be told twice. Tommy and I sat down and ate with them.

Billy said, "This is great, thank you so much."

Rosie spoke up, "Yes, thank you. Do you eat like this every day?"

Shanda told them, "Yes, every day we have at least two meals and sometimes three. You'll get fat in no time." Shanda noticed how skinny they were but didn't press the issue. Shanda used to be skinny like them before she came to live with us. She knows what hunger feels like.

Kendra spoke up, "We eat a lot of fish, fruit, and eggs."

After everyone had eaten our wives took the newly arrived children upstairs to clean them up and provide them new clothes. The ladies of the house would arrange their sleeping quarters.

I told Amy about the infected cut on Peter's foot and that he needed to see the Doc right away. Amy advised me, "After we clean them up we'll all go to the clinic and have them checked out."

Ron approached me and said, "We have to talk about the spy situation."

"Ok, what's up?" I replied.

"Last night someone tried to kill Rick. He got shot in the arm. He's ok but will be out of action for a while. Doc Scott took out a 380 slug. They shot him through the window at his house."

"Shit, that's serious. Everyone likes Rick so who the hell would shoot him? I think from now on we need to post security at our house 24-7 and no one goes anywhere by themselves. I'm done playing around with these spies."

I phoned Rick and asked, "I just got back from my recon and heard someone shot you. Are you ok and do you know who did it?"

"I'm ok. It's lucky for me they were a bad shot. I just worry it could have been my wife or daughter. I don't know who did it. The Doc told me it was a 380 round. If I was going to kill someone I wouldn't use that round."

I told Rick, "I got an idea who shot you. There's only one person I know who carries a 380 semi-auto and that's Scotty."

"Who's that?"

"You know Scotty, he works in the fields for Maggie and Farmer John."

"Oh that Scotty. I call him Scott. You think he did it?"

"We need to get the slug from Doc and do a ballistics check on it then get Scotty's gun and compare the two."

"Good idea, Jack."

"Listen Rick I'm going to call Maggie and find out where Scotty is. We'll grab him on the spot and check his gun today. You call Doc and get that bullet from him. Once you got it let me know."

I called Maggie on her phone and asked her, "Maggie, have you seen Scotty today?"

She replied, "Yep, he's out here picking vegetables now. Why? Do you want to talk to him?"

"Yes, but I'm coming down there now to meet him face to face. Don't tell him I called. You got that Maggie."

"Ya, I got it Jack."

I told Tommy, "Let's go pick up Scotty at the farm. Maggie told me he was there. We'll surprise him and take his gun for ballistics analysis." The sun had come up and it appeared to be around 8 am.

As we were driving to the farm I asked Tommy, "What did you find at the Dali?"

"We couldn't get close enough to see inside because of all the guards. It seems that they're still making BOTs because workers were loading something into a big truck. I think they're taking them to fight SOCOM. Willis also thinks that Sessions will order an air strike to blow up the Dali and stop the production of the BOTs. Some innocent people may be killed but that happens in war."

We drove past the Army check point into no-mans-land where our farm was located. Our farm covers twenty acres. We grow all types of beans, corn, berries, basically anything green. We have forty people who do the picking and tending of the crops. Maggie is in charge of farming and receives help from Farmer John and Victor Elway, our two old-time farmers.

We saw Maggie driving the tractor down the road and upon seeing us she stopped. I asked her,

"Where's Scotty at?"

"He's over there by the fence picking berries. Come on, I'll show you. It's a short walk. By the way what do you want him for?"

"I think he shot Rick last night and I want to check his gun."

"Why would he shoot Rick? Is Rick ok?"

"Yep, Rick is ok. We think Scotty is a Fed spy."

"You mean a spy like Guy and his friends who you killed yesterday? You know Jack everyone is saying you over stepped your bounds. The rumor is you killed them in cold blood. You just gunned them down in the street."

"Thanks for telling me what people are saying. We're going to call a meeting to explain what happened. We couldn't tell everyone on Tocabaga what was going on. Trying to find out who's a spy had to be kept a secret."

"Wow, I would have never expected that from Scotty. He pretty much keeps to himself but come to think of it he does bitch a lot about how things are run on Tocabaga."

"There you go, he's a shoe-in."

"Jack, are you going to kill him?"

"If he puts up a fight we'll have to kill him."

"Jack, let me arrest him. I hate spies and I trusted him all along. I'd love to get him back. He's been getting pretty bossy lately. He thinks he owns me for some reason and is always following me around. He gives me the creeps and I thought about killing him myself."

I had long suspected that Scotty was trying to get in good with Maggie ever since her husband Robbie was killed in a battle against the Feds. Scotty was assigned to the fishing crew but changed to become a farmer after Robbie's death. He was always around Maggie asking if she needed anything fixed. He followed her around like a dog in heat and it was obvious he was trying to make it with her. I knew Maggie and that would never happen because Robbie never liked Scotty.

Tommy and I looked at each other and he said, "Why not let her arrest him. We can cover her and he won't expect her to pull a gun on him. When he sees us he might start shooting or try to run."

Scotty is not a dummy or a little guy. Put it this way; I would think twice before fighting him.

You never know what he is thinking and he has that kind of crazy-looking face. His head looks like a box. It's almost square in shape and is probably hard as a rock. He has some facial scars which means he's been in a few fights. He moved here six years ago from north Florida and other than that I know nothing about him. He has no wife or kids. I heard a rumor he had a dishonorable discharge from the Navy. I classify him as a dangerous person.

"Maggie, we'll back you up. Walk up to him and immediately draw your gun and we'll run in and grab him. Don't stand close to him. Stand about ten feet away when you pull your gun. If he reaches in his pocket or waist band shoot him three times. You got that?"

Maggie always carries a subcompact 9 mm Glock 26 on her hip. She is never without a gun.

"Ok Jack … you wait by the edge of the corn field about 50 yards away and when I draw my gun you guys come running."

Hiding on the edge of the corn field we watched Maggie walk up to Scotty. Tommy had his M4 aimed at Scotty's back and would shoot him if he made a move for a weapon.

Maggie and Scotty started talking to each

other when suddenly Maggie drew her pistol and shot him three times.

I asked Tommy, "Did he go for his gun?"

"I couldn't tell exactly from here."

Tommy and I ran over to her. She was standing over Scotty still pointing the gun at him but he was dead meat. Three bullet holes were in his body. There was one in the head and two in the chest. She did a triple tap just like I taught her to do years ago when learning how to shoot.

Years ago when I sensed the country was changing for the worst, I started training women how to shoot and fight so they could defend themselves against any evil-doers. I started training Amy, my daughter first, and then Maggie and Trini wanted to be trained. Slowly but surely other women became interested in self-defense. Now we have a select group of twenty women warriors who can shoot with the best. They train every week at the farm. I call them the Amazon Warriors and believe me you don't want to mess with any of them. They would cut your balls off and hand them to you on a plate.

The legendary Amazon Warriors are believed to have lived in a part of modern day Turkey. There they formed an independent all-

woman kingdom ruled by a Queen. They were also called the Androktones or killers of men. No men were permitted to reside in Amazon country. Once a year to prevent their race from dying out, they would visit a neighboring tribe. Any male children who were born from these visits were killed or sent back to their fathers. The girls were brought up by their mothers and trained in the art of war. When they went to war men would be taken as slaves or killed. When they grew tired of a man he would be killed or forced to leave their country.

I told her, "Maggie, you can put your gun away; now he's dead. What happen, why did you shoot him?"

"I had no choice, Jack, he called me a fucking bitch when I told him he was a fucking spy. I don't take that from anybody." Maggie wasn't supposed to tell him she knew he was a spy.

"Did he go for his gun?"

"I think he did."

"Don't say that. You know he went for his gun. Ok Maggie you saved us the trouble." I bent down took the 380 Colt Mustang out of Scotty's pocket.

I stood up and put my arm around Maggie

giving her a hug. She returned the hug, patted me on the chest, and said, "Thanks for the hug, Jack, but I'm ok."

Tommy ran over and got his truck. He tied a rope around Scotty's legs and dragged the body thru the weeds to the beach about 200 feet away. Tommy rolled the body into the water so it would never to be seen again as the current would wash it out to sea.

As I got in the truck to leave, I told Maggie, "It was self-defense just remember that. We both saw him go for his gun. Stop over at the house some time if you want to talk. You're welcome at our place anytime."

"Ok Jack, maybe we can have a drink sometime. See y'all later. Hey be careful out there!" I waved as we drove away to obtain the bullet from Rick for ballistics analysis.

We pulled up to Rick's house and he came outside when he saw our truck. I told him, "Scotty is dead and here's his gun. Maggie shot him in self-defense when we tried to arrest him. By the way, did you look around for the spent shell casing?"

Rick replied, "I hope the bullets match his gun, otherwise Maggie shot the wrong guy."

"I told you it was self-defense. He went for his gun. We saw the whole thing."

"Ok, Jack, if you say so. By the way what will the shell casing tell you?"

"Every gun makes a firing pin mark on the casing so if we can find it we'll fire this gun and compare the two casings. It'll save us a lot of ballistics work."

"He shot me from the front yard so it's gotta be around here somewhere."

I've always been lucky at finding something that was lost in the sand or weeds. We walked around searching for about 45 minutes. It was a hot day so I stopped and took off my hat to wipe the sweat from my head. While wiping off my face I closed my eyes and a picture popped into my head. It was a picture of the casing in the dirt next to my shoe. I opened my eyes as I looked down and there it was right next to my shoe. That's not the first time I've had visions. I get these visions or pictures in my head when I close my eyes while searching for something. They just pop up showing the missing object's location. I know it sounds weird but it's true.

I yelled, "Holy shit here's the shell right next to my foot! Let's fire a round now and compare them." I chambered a round and fired it into the ground. The spent shell ejected out and Tommy caught it in mid air before it even hit the ground. He has great reflexes.

We huddled together as I held both shells up next to each other. It was clear they were a match. There was no doubt that this gun was used to shoot Rick. Rick commented, "That sure looks like a match to me. Good work guys."

Tommy replied, "No doubt Scotty was the guy that shot you."

I advised Rick, "We need to have a general meeting and tell the people what has been going on. Maggie told me that a lot of people are upset because we killed GA and his buddies the other day. The problem is no one knows they were spies and now we need to bring it out in the open. No one knows we shot them in self-defense.

"If there are more spies here we'll make it clear we are searching for them and justice will be swift. Maybe that will scare them into submission and they'll cease any more spy activity."

"I agree, Jack, and I'll set up a meeting for tonight at the fire circle at 6 pm. You'll do all the talking."

"Ok with me. I'll see you later."

As Tommy and I left my phone rang, it was Sessions. "Jack, I just finished going over the recon data with Willis and Hammer. We are planning to attack the Dome tonight and I've asked SOCOM to bomb the Dali. We'll depart here at 2300 hours.

SOCOM will bomb the factory at midnight at the same time we attack the Dome. Do you have the spy situation under control?"

"We killed another spy today. He shot Rick in the arm last night and he had to be terminated. So far we've killed 5 spies and I still think there are a few more. I think Johnny is a spy but I don't have any proof. We're going to have a general meeting tonight at 6 pm to tell everyone what's going on. Once the cat is out of the bag I think any remaining spies will cease their activities, leave Tocabaga, or if we find out who they are they'll go on trial."

"Well, I'm going to need all my men to raid the Dome and rescue my Rangers. I require your assistance to guard the Fort while we're gone. You'll need to keep alert since we are taking both BVFs' but I will leave the Iron Maiden here guarding the main bridge. I want you to post ten men at the Fort HQ and two at the entrance until we come back."

BFV means Bradley Fighting Vehicle. The Bradley M3 Fighting Vehicle, named after General Omar Bradley from WWII, has a three-member crew. It weighs in at 27 tons, and is fully armored. It fires a 25mm chain gun which can destroy most tanks and has a 7.62 M240 machine gun to mow down ground troops if needed.

"Captain, that's not a problem I'll assign my Amazon Warriors to that duty."

"Amazon Warriors, who are they?"

"It's a long story but I trained a group of women years ago who can shoot with the best and they're tough as nails. They would really like to pull guard duty. I trust them with my life. You've probably seen them training near the farm every weekend."

"Yes I have seen them but I just thought they were a bunch of women working out. You know trying to stay in shape." I laughed at that comment.

"Have your Amazon Warriors report for duty at 2100 hours. Willis and Hammer will fill them in on the details."

"Yes sir, at 2100 hours sharp. See you then, Captain."

My Amazon Warriors have not seen any action so far. They want to be on the front line and do their share. This guard duty will really give them a boost in morale because they're doing something important. I'll call Maggie, Amy, and Trini and ask them to have their squad assembled for the meeting tonight. I want to show them off and use them for added security patrols on Tocabaga to prevent any more assassination attempts by the so-called spies.

Maggie was the wife of my buddy Robbie who was killed by the Feds. Maggie is 38 years old and works out all the time. She once killed an ex-con years ago, who broke into their house. She is one tough cookie and an excellent shot. Maggie is in charge of all the farming that supports our community.

Trini is a married woman who works for Maggie on the farm. She's in great shape and can out run most men. She likes knife fighting and is always begging me to give her more lessons. She has good eye - hand coordination and is excellent in hand-to-hand combat because of her fast reflexes.

My daughter Amy has trained with me since she was 7 years old. She started shooting when she was 10 years old. She has a black belt in judo and has studied Jeet Kune Do for over 10 years. Amy is 5'11" tall and is a lean mean fighting machine. All of the Amazon women are beautiful and shapely but they're also deadly.

My warriors wear Army digital camouflage uniforms with black combat boots and bullet proof vests but no hats. Instead of a hat they wear a black bandana head band. Each one is assigned an M4 carbine that has a 4x ACOG or Advanced Combat Optical Gun Sight. The three commanders also carry a 9 mm Glock 26 subcompact handgun on their tactical combat vests. All of them carry one unique item to set them apart which is an 18 inch long Barong-style machete in a black scabbard hanging from their waist like a sword.

The M4 carbine was derived from earlier versions of the M16 rifle, which was in turn a copy the original AR15 rifle. The M4 is shorter and lighter than the M16A2 assault rifle. It is a gas operated magazine-fed, shoulder fired weapon with a telescoping stock and 14.5 in barrel. It fires the .223 caliber, or 5.56mm NATO round.

Barong Machetes are known for their thick leaf-shaped blade which is sharp on both sides. It was the traditional weapon of certain tribes in the Philippines. The Barong was feared by European colonizers because it was so deadly. The shape allows one to slash or stab. The blade is so sharp and strong it can cut your arm off with one swing. The Barong is one scary weapon.

I'm going to have the Warriors march into the meeting in formation and stand there watching over the whole proceedings. I want the traitors to know that we have a new group of warriors they will have to contend with. I am trying to scare them into submission. The Amazon women will be the protectors of Tocabaga, much like a police force. They'll watch our homes and help us find out who else may be a traitor.

I told my three commanders, Amy, Trini, and Maggie, to assemble the group behind the bank at 5:50 pm. They would march out to the fire ring when the meeting starts at 6 pm and line up directly behind me. The only people who know about the Amazon Warriors are the Board members and my security team leaders. It was going to be a sight to behold.

Six o'clock came around and there were an estimated 100 people in attendance for the meeting. That attendance is slightly more than normal.

Rick stood up and said, "I hereby call this meeting to order. Jack is going to advise everyone on our current situation. First we'll say the Pledge of Allegiance." We say the Pledge at every meeting so we don't forget who we are and we teach it to our children.

Everyone stood up putting their right hand over their heart, looked at the flag waving in the breeze, and repeated in unison, "*I pledge allegiance to the Flag of the United States of America, and to the Republic for which it stands, one Nation under God, indivisible, with liberty and justice for all.*"

Every time we do this as a group it sends

chills down my spine. I glanced around to see who was repeating the pledge and noticed that the suspected spies were not saying the pledge. To me that's a big clue as to who isn't a Patriot.

Shortly after the Pledge you could hear the sound of the Amazon Warriors marching in lock step. You could hear their boots making one unified noise. Everyone turned around to observe the women warriors march in with M4 carbines slung over their shoulders on a 3 point Specter tactical sling, and Barong machetes hanging from their belts. All of them in matching uniforms, marching in perfect formation.

They marched up right behind me and the Board members.

Amy yelled, "Squad halt! ... Squad at ease!"

I stood up and advised the crowd, "These are the Amazon Warriors. You know these women. They are part of our community. They have been training very hard and are now ready to do their part in providing security for Tocabaga. These women will be patrolling the streets of Tocabaga day and night. They have full authority to stop and detain anyone whom they deem suspicious."

Most people started to clap, some even whistled, and cheered, but some I could tell were not happy. I proceeded with my speech. "We have spies and traitors on Tocabaga. That is why Guy Allen and his buddies were killed the other day. We found out they were sending messages to the Feds and when we confronted them a gun battle broke out. They went for their guns and we had no choice but to defend ourselves. Last night Scotty shot Rick in the arm trying to kill him at his house. Scotty is no longer with us either."

Someone yelled, "Jack, you killed 5 people in two days. What gives you the right to do that?" The voice was Troy's and standing near him was Chase and Johnny. These are the people I suspected of being spies.

Looking Troy in the eyes I continued in a loud voice, "I don't know if there are more traitors living here or not but if there is … make no mistake we will find you. You will pay for committing treason.

"You ask me what gives me the right to shoot someone. It's called the Stand Your Ground Law. If someone draws a gun, or points one at me, or if I deem them a threat to my life, I can use deadly force. You got any other stupid questions, Troy?" Troy and his buddies were silent.

"Now I'd like you to meet three kids I found living just outside the green zone." The kids stood up for everyone to see.

"This is Rosie, she is fifteen years old, Billy is thirteen, and Peter is nine years old. Take a good look at them. These are children who need our protection and love. The Feds shot their parents for stealing food in the Green Zone and then threw them out of the zone to the wolves. They were living on the streets with no one to help them. Every day they had to search for food just to stay alive. Now they're living here on Tocabaga with my family. This could have happened to your kids if you lived in the Green Zone."

I touched each child on the head and Hemmi then took the children home for the night. Tonight they could sleep unafraid knowing that someone was taking care of them.

"If you think the Feds have the answers then go live in the Green Zone. Leave now and don't come back to Tocabaga. The Federal Government and the President who declared Executive Order 13603 are the ones that screwed up our country. It declares that all property belongs to the Federal Government; your house, money, guns, and even your kids. They can tell you where to live and where to work. They're the ones that violated the Bill of Rights and the Constitution as a whole."

"If you want the type of government that tells you what to do all the time then leave now. We'll give you a ride if you need it. There won't be any hard feelings, just leave.

"But beware, if you stay here on Tocabaga and commit treason you will pay a huge price when I find out who you are. I can promise justice will be swift and painful."

Johnny shouted, "I'm sick and tired of your shit, Jack. You think you're the King here. You got your own Army now and you're telling us what to do!"

Chase and Troy both shouted, "He's right! King Jack, long live the King!"

Rick butted into the disagreement, "Everyone here voted us in office. If you don't like it leave. It's a mean world out there! I know one thing. If it wasn't for Jack setting up the original defense for Tocabaga we'd all be slaves to the Feds or dead by now. Jack has risked his life many times for the good of Tocabaga."

Chris stood up and commented, "Johnny, if you don't like it, then get the hell out of Tocabaga. I was there at the bridge when the doper gang attacked us. It was Jack that saved many of us from being killed that day."

Some others yelled, "Chris is right." That shut up Johnny and his buddies.

You can't argue with a progressive socialist because they won't listen to reason or common sense. These QUISLINGS want to run Tocabaga themselves. They're the ones that want the power and control over the people. They're the ones that want the glory. They're the ones who want to be the Kings. They try to fool the people by using words like Peoples Party, Republic, and the all famous word Socialist. They always say things like "it's for the good of the people."

(The term Quisling was coined by the a British newspaper in an editorial published on April 19, 1940, entitled "Quislings Everywhere" after Vidkun Quisling, who assisted Nazi Germany to conquer his own country so that he could rule the government himself. Hence, it means a traitor or spy who wants to be in control.)

Look at the following three examples how the people were fooled.

The Union of Soviet Socialist Republics, the USSR was a socialist state between 1922 and 1991. It was governed as a single-party state by the Communist Party. Millions of people starved to death or were sent to prison for not being a good Commie. People lived and worked where the state told them to.

China is officially the People's Republic of China. It's the world's most populous country with a population of over 1.35 billion. It is a Communist/Socialist state, single-party system. The people really have no control over their own lives or property even if it is called the People's Republic. Millions were killed during and after their civil war by the good commie leaders. The people have no power at all.

Nazi Germany, or the Third Reich, are common names for Germany during the period from 1933 to 1945, when its government was controlled by Adolf Hitler and his National SOCIALIST German Workers' Party or Nazi Party. Under Hitler's rule, Germany was transformed into a Fascist totalitarian government which controlled nearly all aspects of life. Hitler became dictator of Germany when the powers of the Chancellery and Presidency were merged. Hitler's word was above all laws. Hitler once wrote the bigger lie you tell the more people will believe it.

Rick stood up saying, "The meeting is adjourned there is nothing else to discuss."

People started leaving and I noticed that the three amigos were leaving together with one other person who was waiting for them in the shadows. I couldn't identify him so I asked Rick, "Who's that guy with Johnny?"

"I don't know. I can't tell from here," Rick replied.

"It means Johnny has some allies and that means more trouble."

I asked Tommy to follow them discretely, at a safe distance, to see where they go. I wanted him to identify the stranger with Johnny. Since Tommy was a sniper he could sneak around pretty well without being noticed.

Thirty minutes later Tommy reported back to me. He didn't know who the other guy was but they went to Johnny's boat. Johnny lives on a 48 foot fishing boat and doesn't own a house. The boat is anchored near shark channel close to the old Tampa Bay Watch house. Unfortunately, this is also close to the bridge that goes to Fort Desoto and they could monitor movement in and out of the Fort.

I advised Tommy, "I could be wrong but I think he's a Fed agent that has infiltrated here. When Johnny goes fishing no one goes with him. He could pick up some agents and bring them here with no one ever knowing it."

"Yep, it's possible Dad since he docks his boat near the bridge to the Fort where no one can see him. He's off the grid so to speak. What do you want to do now?"

"You go back to the boat and keep an eye on

them. If they move give me a call. I'm going to tell Ron and Jim Bo to be ready because we may have trouble brewing. We'll be roving between the Fort and the main bridge.

"The Amazon Warriors go on duty at the Fort at 2100 hours. Two will be guarding the bridge and ten at the Rangers HQ. That leaves eight for patrolling the rest of Tocabaga."

It was almost 2100 hours so the Amazon squad would be reporting to Sergeant Willis at the Fort. I had informed the remaining eight, under the command of Trini, to start patrolling the north and south ends of Tocabaga.

It was 2300 hours and the Rangers were leaving for their rescue mission. I was standing on the side of the road when Captain Sessions pulled up to me. He advised us that Corporal Phillips, the radio man, would remain at the Fort.

We followed the convoy to the main bridge and watched them disappear into the darkness. My phone rang; it was Tommy. "I got bad news. Five men just left the boat with Johnny and they are armed with rifles and one has an RPG."

"Shit. An RPG? Well, now we know these guys aren't local people. We'll have to take them out. Where are they going Tommy?"

"It looks like they're headed toward Troy's

place."

"I wonder what these guys are planning to do. If they hook up with Troy and Chase then there'll be eight of them. If we hadn't killed five already we'd be up against thirteen of them."

"Dad, whatever their plan is it doesn't matter. We need to arrest them now," urged Tommy.

"All right, keep following them and once they're at Troy's house let me know. I'll get the Amazons and with Jim Bo and Ron we'll surround the house."

The eight warriors under the command of Trini met us a block away from Troy's house. I advised them the plan was to surround the house. Then we would call them out. If they don't come out of the house we would open fire. I explained one man has an RPG so it was imperative to take that guy out.

An RPG is a rocket propelled grenade. It is a shoulder fired weapon system that fires rockets equipped with an explosive warhead. An RPG can blow up a car or shoot down a helicopter.

I received a phone call as we were moving

into position around the house. It was the Corporal Phillips, "I just received another message over the CB radio. The message reads; *Ranger convoy just left Tocagaba headed your way putting plan in action Jones.* So you better be ready for something, Jack."

"Ok. Thanks a lot Phillips."

I told my team another coded message was sent tipping off the Feds that the Rangers left the Fort. These guys are QUISLINGS and if they don't surrender shoot to kill.

We had the house covered, the women fighters were on the east and west sides of the house. Jim Bo with Ron moved to the south side where the back door was located. Tommy and I were at the north side covering the main door.

I yelled, "Troy! You and your gang come out with your hands in the air! You're all under arrest for treason!" There was no reply.

I shouted again, "You have 5 minutes to come out or we'll open fire!"

It was dark out but we could see inside the house there was a dim light coming from a candle. The candle went out and all of a sudden an RPG zoomed out the open window at Tommy and me. We ducked behind our truck. It blew the truck up and the force of the explosion knocked us to the ground. We were dazed from the explosion and the truck started to burn. The fire lit up the dark night allowing them to see our movements.

Now, rapid gunfire was coming from inside the house. To escape the heat of the burning truck Tommy moved to the left and I moved to the right as we opened fire on full automatic. I dove behind a couple of big rocks and Tommy jumped behind a tree. Now all my warriors were firing into the house.

The dirtbags inside were trying to return fire but I knew that would be difficult to do as our bullets were shooting right through the thin walls of the old house. I could see Trini on the west side of the house with her team hiding behind a wooden fence. Then I saw an RPG round slam into the fence. Trini, along with her three girls, went flying backwards as the fence blew apart. I was worried that some of them might have been killed.

I didn't see the two men who jumped out of the west side window, and started to run toward the blown up fence, until they were almost on top of Trini. Trini was laying on the ground stunned. One man had the RPG and the other carried a rifle.

I took aim at the dork with the RPG and fired a burst knocking him to the ground. The man with the rifle shot two warriors at close range and turned his gun on Trini. Trini was in the line of fire so I didn't have a clear shot. Trini jumped up like a cat with no gun in her hand … the spy aimed his weapon and pulled the trigger but nothing happened it was jammed or empty.

He reached in his pocket for another magazine. Trini pulled out her Barong machete and like a tigress sprang thru the air before he could reload. With one swift swing she split his head open, cutting it in half like a ripe melon. He fell to the ground with brains sliding out of his skull.

Trini picked up her M4 and continued firing into the house while laying on the ground. Tommy yelled at me and I turned to look at him. He signaled he was going to throw a hand grenade inside the house. He stood up and from 20 feet away tossed it in an open window. There was a giant flash and … KABOOM … the bomb exploded.

During a fire fight the noise from the gunfire is incredible. You can hardly hear a damn thing with 12 guns going off. I yelled to Trini as loud as I could, "Cease fire. Pass it on." I gave her the standard hand signal waving my hand near my throat which means stop.

There was a slight amount of return fire still coming from the house. I told Tommy to throw another grenade in the east-side window. It exploded and then all was silent.

Tommy shouted to me, "Let's go in!" We slowly approached the front door. Tommy entered first and I followed close behind him. If my count was correct there were eight men in the house to start. There were two dead outside and we found five more dead in various rooms.

I told Tommy, "There's one man missing and I think it's Troy." We continued searching the house.

Tommy yelled, "Here's the scumbag in the main bathroom." I ran to the room and Troy was in the bath tub. That's how he stayed alive from all the gunfire. The bullets bounced off the old cast iron tub protecting him from any harm.

Troy was holding up his hands begging, "Please don't kill me." I grabbed him by the shirt, dragged him outside, and threw him on the ground. Then for good measure I kicked him in the head and told him to shut up.

Trini walked up to me with tears in her eyes and said, "Jack, two of my girls are dead." I walked over to them and checked their pulse just to make sure. I saw that both had been shot in the head.

They died in the line of combat. These were the first women to be killed on Tocabaga. I made the sign of the cross as Jim Bo went to the truck and picked up two body bags. We carefully placed their warrior bodies inside the bags and carried them to the pickup truck.

I checked Trini for wounds because she had blood covering her face and hands. There were wood splitters embedded in her skin from the fence blowing up. Linda, the other Amazon on Trini's team, who was at the fence, had the same injuries. They're not serious wounds but I'm sure they were painful. I told them both to go to the Clinic when we were finished here.

Ron was guarding Troy who wasn't even wounded. Trini ran over to Troy and kicked him multiple times. She screamed, "You fucking shit head traitor. I want to kill you!"

Linda came over and started kicking Troy. I let them kick the shit out of him. They had to vent their anger. They had to let it all out rather than keep it inside and have mental problems later. The other four Amazon Warriors also walked up to Troy and each one took turns venting their anger by kicking Troy who now appeared to be knocked out. I let them have their way because Troy deserved it.

My men and I just stood there watching the beating take place. After a few minutes I said, "Ok warriors, he's knocked out. He can't feel anything. We'll take him to the Fort and lock him up. He'll be held there until we put him on trial."

"Let us lock his ass up," Trini asked.

I thought about it for a minute and replied, "Ok, go ahead, but don't kick him anymore. He'll get his justice."

They loaded his unconscious body into the back of a pickup and took off for the Fort. I had a feeling that Troy would never make it to trial. Somehow he would meet his maker at the hands of the Amazon Warriors. Too bad for Troy but I didn't really care what happened to him. I knew better than to piss off the women warriors. Two of their sisters had just been killed in their first combat so emotions were running high.

I felt remorse for the two warriors' deaths. Maybe I shouldn't have assigned them the duty. Maybe they needed more experience. Maybe it was really my fault they died.

Checking the time it was 2 am. We searched the house and found another CB radio inside. That proved that Troy was a Quisling. We checked the other bodies and found ID badges hanging around their necks proving the five men were Federal agents working undercover to take over Tocabaga.

An hour later we were dragging the bodies to the seawall to toss them to the sharks when my phone rang. It was Trini speaking in an excited voice. "Jack … Troy tried to escape so we had to shoot him."

"I'm not surprised Trini, don't worry about it, just throw his body into Shark Channel."

I advised my men that Troy was just killed trying to escape. Jim Bo said, "Escape? I don't think he could walk after the beating they gave him. Even if he could run where would he go? He couldn't get off the island."

"I don't know Jim, but there is nothing we can do about his death. Furthermore, I don't want to hear any more about it. You guys go to the Fort and check what's going on. Oh, and on the way there check out Johnny's boat for any weapons. I'm going home to bed."

The fact is anyone of us could have been killed tonight. We have to be more careful. We need to improve our security and maybe the Amazon Warriors are just what we need. We have to make Tocabaga a safer place.

Captain Sessions hasn't come back yet from the rescue mission. I hoped all was going well. I was very tired because this was my second night without sleep. I can't keep working 24 hours a day; it'll get me killed. When you're fatigued you can't think clearly and your reflexes slow down.

JUNE 29, 2025

My phone was ringing and I looked at the clock it was 9 am. Sessions was calling me so I answered, "Hello Captain."

"Hello Jack, just calling you to let you know everything went as planned. We rescued four Rangers and retrieved four bodies. We also brought Carl back with us. Come on down for a coffee and I'll tell you the whole story. I also want to hear what happened to the spies."

"Ok Captain give me an hour and I'll be there."

I took a shower and dressed. I went downstairs for some coffee and food. My wife told me, "Jack there are a lot of women waiting outside for you."

"Women? What do they want?"

Ron answered, "They all want to become Amazon Warriors." Ron, Tommy, and Jim Bo started to laugh. It seems the deaths of Jill and Sally spurred more women into wanting to be of service. They all wanted to be Amazon Warriors.

"They need to talk to Amy, not me. Where is she?" Just then Amy entered the room.

"Amy you need to talk to the women outside because they all want to be Warriors."

"Ok I will, but we only need to replace two women. I wanted to tell you what happened to Troy last night. Trini and Linda took him to the guard house and then I heard gunfire. I ran over there but Troy was dead. They told me he tried to escape so they shot him about 20 times. That's all I know."

"Ok thanks for the information but Trini all ready told me. Maybe their story is true and maybe it's not. At this point what difference does it make? I'm not going to question their story. The main thing is the spies are dead."

I put on my bullet proof vest while thinking about the situation and holstered my Glock 17. I chugged some coffee and telling Amy. "I want you to have the warriors patrol Tocabaga day and night 24-7. Have four women on a patrol at one time. Any boats that go fishing are to be inspected when they come back to the dock. If something seems out of the ordinary report back to me."

"Ok. Will do, Dad."

"I don't think we have anymore spies here but the boats need to be checked. That was a weak point that I missed. We need the Warriors to be our police on the island. They'll be our eyes and ears keeping a sharp look out so we're all safe.

"You'll have to arrange the funeral of your two warriors. Have the service at two pm and post a notice on the bulletin board. I suggest that Trini, Maggie, and you be the honor guard. You'll need to perform the service. Was Sally or Jill married?"

"Sally was married so her husband Wayne will speak at the service. Jill wasn't married, but her best friend was Trini so she'll say some words. I already spoke to them about it."

"I would like to speak at the service also. So you start it off and then let me speak and then the others. Jim Bo will use his boat to take the bodies out to sea with Wayne, Maggie, Trini, and you after the service. Be sure that all your girls are there in full uniform and they'll do a 21 gun salute on your command."

"Ok, will do. Now I'm going to talk to the volunteers waiting outside."

"See you at the funeral service. I have to go see Sessions now." I asked my men to come with me to the Fort for the meeting.

It was going to be another busy hot day on Tocabaga. We drove to the Fort to have a meeting with Captain Sessions. I filled him in on the spy situation and the fact we lost two women warriors in a gun battle. He felt very sorry about that and was surprised when I told him that there were five FBI agents on Tocabaga who apparently came here on Johnny's boat. I explained how the Amazons would be patrolling 24-7 and inspecting all boats when they return from fishing trips. If there are any others inclined to be spies, that will make them think twice.

Sessions then filled us in on what happened on the rescue mission. They blitzed the Dome with the BVFs and the Humvees destroying five Federal trucks. The Bradleys blew open the Dome doors and his men rushed inside killing all the guards.

While this was going on his two Blackhawks flew over and destroyed two more trucks loaded with men using the M134 mini Gatling guns. Two SOCOM fighter planes bombed the Dali at the same time wiping it off the map.

The M134 Minigun is a 7.62x51 mm NATO,

six-barreled Gatling gun with a high rate of fire up to 6,000 rounds per minute. It has rotating barrels with an external electric motor. This baby shoots a steam of fire that can cut trees in half.

Inside they found four Rangers still alive and four bodies. Along with them was Carl, Jr. and an estimated 200 other prisoners. They all wanted to be let out but there was no way of telling who was a political prisoner and who was a real criminal. Sessions didn't have time to interrogate them and he couldn't bring them back to Tocabaga. He unlocked all the cells telling the people they were free to leave. Only God knows where they went to.

One Father with two little kids begged Sessions to take his kids even if he couldn't come along. Sessions rescued all three of them bringing them to Tocabaga. Too sum it up there were no fatalities but one Ranger was slightly wounded. The mission was a success.

Sessions commented, "After we're finished here I'll introduce you to Albert Madison and his two boys. You can take him under your wing and find them a place to live. He seems like an ok guy. He claims he was in the Navy for eight years. We're doing a background check on him now."

It turned out that Albert Madison was a

Navy Corpsman and Tommy knew him from the Korean War in 2018. Navy Corpsmen serve as combat medics for the Marines. Combat medics are a Marines' best friend. Albert's security clearance wouldn't be a problem. We can always use another medic here on Tocabaga.

I stated, "Of course we'll help out Mr. Madison. How is it going at SOCOM?"

"The major battle is over and the Federal troops have been defeated except for a few pockets. I have been ordered to deploy my Rangers to cut off any forces trying to escape. It's just a mop up job. Tonight we will move against them using the two Bradleys and the Iron Maiden. That leaves you with no armor for security but we'll only be gone for a few days."

The Iron Maiden is the name of the Abrams tank commanded by Captain Riley who is also a very close friend of Captain Sessions.

The M1A2 Abrams Tank is named after General Abrams. It fires a whopping 120mm laser aimed cannon and never misses its target. The cannon can blow up buildings or other tanks. It has one M2 50 Caliber Heavy Machine Gun, and two 7.62 M240 machine guns. Bullets and other large projectiles just bounce off the sides of this big boy.

I advised Sessions, "I guess it's a good thing I have the Amazon Warriors activated. We'll have to put the road block on the bridge again and start full 24-7 security."

"Jack, you will also need ten people here at the Fort for security."

"Ok, I'll keep the Warriors out here. How soon are you deploying?"

"We'll roll out of here at 2100 hours."

"All right. My warriors will be here by 2000 hours. We have a funeral service today at 1400 hours."

I wasn't happy about the Rangers leaving for two days or longer. We all felt secure with the Rangers here. Even a small force of Rangers is appreciated by the people living here. Sessions and I walked outside and found Albert Madison and his two boys, who appeared to be 13 to 15 years old.

After introductions to my crew I asked Jim Bo to find them a condo to live in and show them around Tocabaga. Jim would also provide them the proper ID name tags to hang around their necks.

Albert Madison was a good-looking stocky-build man. He had long arms and his hands almost hung down to his knees. Long arms means you have some added muscle that normal people of the same height don't have. His two boys looked just like him.

It was a muggy hot day as we all stood at the service for Sally and Jill. The Amazon squad performed the twenty one gun salute and we all listened to the speeches. It was a sad and moving service. Everyone had tears in their eye's as their bodies were covered with a flag and put on the boat. Jim Bo would take the bodies 30 miles off shore. The body bags would be weighted down and then slid overboard while saying "The Lord's Prayer."

On land we have a cemetery across from the church where we place a white cross with the names and dates of those that have died so they will always be remembered. Some of the Tocabaga women place fresh flowers at each cross once a week.

Later that evening all the warriors went to the bar to celebrate the life of Sally and Jill. I warned them not to drink too much because they would be on duty tonight. I went home to spend some time with the family. I thought quality time with the family is important. You never know when it could be your last day here on earth.

That night the Rangers pulled out at 2100 hours and the women warriors went on duty as soon as the Rangers left. We were now on our own with no Ranges here to help protect us from evil.

I needed to rest because there's no telling what could happen tomorrow. I tried not to think about it as I closed my eyes trying to sleep, trying to reach dream land. My dream land is usually nightmare land where I lead an Army made up of dead people.

JUNE 30, 2025

Today we rebuilt the road block to keep vehicles from crossing the bridge into Tocabaga. This is done by interlocking ten cars in an angular "V" shaped pattern thereby creating a wall of cars.

I received an Army gmail, sent to tocabaga.jack, from Sessions advising he would be delayed another 5 to 10 days because of the mop-up operations. This was not good news.

Late in the afternoon a group of twenty people came walking up the road to the bridge. They were asking for food and were demanding that we let them cross the bridge to live here.

One man stepped forward and yelled, "You have to let us in. You don't own this island. You didn't build this. You need to share what you have." It seems I've heard something similar to that before.

I walked down the bridge right up to the man with the big mouth bringing along Tommy and Jim Bo for back up because a few of them had guns. I stepped up close to him and asked, "Sir, what's your name?"

He replied, "My name is Stan Gill. Who are you?"

"I'm Jack Gunn Director of Security for Tocabaga. Mr. Gill, you don't know it but we do own this island. Most people have been living here more than ten years and paid for these homes. We did create this island sanctuary. We've worked hard to build this up and some have died to protect it. Usually we let people join us after we do a background check. You have a large group of people and it may take some time to check all of you out."

"What do you mean a background check?"

"Camp Tocabaga is a part of an Army Ranger base located here and therefore everyone who wants to live here must submit to an identity check. We need to know if anyone has a criminal history of any kind. We use fingerprints and facial recognition methods which we compare to law enforcement records."

"That seems a little too much if you ask me. You guys aren't cops."

"Actually some of us are cops. Look, we need to protect this island and no one comes in without a background check. If you agree we can arrange to start the process."

"How long does it take?"

"It could take two to ten days."

"What do we do in the meantime? We don't have any cars so traveling is a big problem. We walked here from the Dome. The Rangers raided it yesterday and told us about this so called Tocabaga Island."

"You were prisoners at the Dome?"

"Yes. We're hungry and need shelter. Please help us out, we have no place to go."

I looked at Stan Gill and he didn't look like someone who had been in prison. He didn't look like the others because he was to clean-looking. He had his black hair slicked back in a neat fashion. His face was clean shaven with no sign of stubble. His clothes seemed a little too neat and clean. Stan was about my height and a little leaner I guessed, putting him at around 170 pounds. He looked strong and well fed but it was his sunglasses that made me wonder about him. They were the type of glasses that a typical agent would wear.

It was clear that Stan Gill was the

spokesperson for this group. I looked around at the group and saw it was made up of some young men, but mostly older men and a few women. They didn't threaten us in anyway so I would agree to provide them some food. Then it occurred to me that Albert Madison was at the Dome and maybe he knows some of these people. Maybe he could vouch for them. I asked Jim Bo to find Albert and bring him to the bridge.

Speaking to Stan I said, "I'll tell you what we can do. First we'll give your group some food. When you're finished eating we can take finger prints, facial photographs, and submit them to the Army for a background check.

"We have one man here, Albert Madison, who was at the Dome. If he vows for your group we'll let you come on Tocabaga until the background check comes back. First we'll do an interview with each person and ask you some key questions. If you come on Tocabaga you cannot bring a weapon with you. We'll keep your weapons until you've been cleared."

My plan was to ask each person in private some key questions to help us determine if they could be a bad apple. The questions are:

Have you ever been convicted of a crime? If so, what was the crime?

Do you believe in the Constitution of the United States?

Do you know The Pledge of Allegiance? If so, recite it.

Do you know the first two amendments in the Bill of Rights? If so, what are they?

Are you a socialist or communist? This is a key question. If they are either one then they will be rejected.

What did you do for a living?

I was talking to Stan when Albert showed up so I asked him, "These people claim they were prisoners in the Dome. Do you know this man or any of these people?"

He looked at Stan, then carefully at the people with him, and replied, "Nope, I don't know him, but I recognize some of the others here. You have to remember there were over 200 people in different cells so I don't know everyone."

I advised my men, "To speed up this process take one person at a time to the High and Dry building. Take their names, picture, fingerprints, and interview them. Once you are finished keep the people under guard in the building until we obtain an Army clearance.

"Ron you run all the information down to

Phillips at the Fort and ask him to process it ASAP."

I looked at Stan and said, "Ok we'll let your group come onto Tocabaga one person at a time. You can all stay in the High and Dry building for now. I expect that it will take two to ten days for results to come back. Stan you're first."

The process was in motion and maybe these twenty or so people will have a new home here on Tocabaga. It's out of my control.

Albert walked up to me and said, "Sorry I couldn't be of more help Jack."

"That's ok, Albert, we've done this before. If they don't pass the security check then back on the street they go. How are you and your boys doing?"

"They're doing great and are working on the farm for Maggie. They like it a lot. They like the fresh air and freedom. I'm working with Doc Scott at the clinic. Jack, I want to ask you something."

"Shoot, Albert, what do you want?"

"My wife and oldest son stayed at our old house and didn't come to the green zone with me. She didn't want to leave her home and be under Federal control.

"I took my youngest sons to the Green Zone

about a year ago because I thought it would be safer for them. It wasn't safer and that's how we ended up in jail. Someone tried to steal our food and I got into a fight. My wife was right. I should have stayed with her. We didn't part on good terms. I'm worried sick about her and my son so I want to bring them here."

"Where does she live?"

"We have a house off 66th Street located on 30th Ave. North. It's not far from the old Mall."

"The Mall … I haven't been up there in years. We went to Ellenton Mall a couple of times and had all kinds of FUBAR. I don't like going near any malls. Do you think she's still living at your house?"

"I don't know but I want to find them if possible so I'm asking for your help. As far as what's at the mall I don't know anything about that."

"Albert what you're asking isn't easy. We would need at least two vehicles and four men. That's a fifteen to twenty mile trip one way. It could be very dangerous and there's no telling what we could run into. I would need volunteers to come along. Let me think about it."

As I walked away from Albert I thought the Mall must be a complete mess. It must be loaded with criminals and gang members. Even going near it we could end up in a big FUBAR. I'll ask Tommy for his opinion. I would like to save his wife and son from certain death but it would be a risky mission. The other fact is the Rangers are not at the Fort so we are short handed.

I headed home for the night. I wanted to see my family and enjoy the grandkids. They always make me laugh and I forget about the dangerous times we are living in. I'll discuss Albert's request with Tommy and the family tomorrow. No more work today.

July 1, 2025

It's almost Independence Day. Independence Day has a special meaning for us because we are free men. We aim to stay independent following the Bill of Rights established by our ancestors and given to us by God. Usually we have a big party and this year we were looking forward to celebrating with the Army Rangers. It seems they'll miss the party this year.

The group that arrived yesterday was living in the High & Dry and all the information had been submitted to the Army for background checks. In the meantime our people would become friends with them by taking the group food and water.

I was sitting on the patio with my family having a cup of coffee and I mentioned Albert's request to search for his wife and oldest son. I explained, "His wife stayed behind to live at their house with his 18 year-old son. Albert moved to the green zone about a year ago with his two youngest boys for safety reasons."

Tonya, my son's wife, stated, "What if she doesn't want to come here to live?"

Tommy commented, "She may be dead for all we know."

"Yep, I know the odds aren't good but since Albert is a veteran we owe him."

"Yes, that's true. I'll go with you."

Amy spoke up, "I'm in also. How many people do you need?"

"I think four people and two trucks."

Amy replied, "I'll ask Maggie if she wants to go along. She's game for anything adventurous."

"Ok ask her. It's eight am so let's plan to leave here by ten am. I'll tell Albert to get ready. Tommy, you get the gear and ammo ready. We'll take the two black SUVs' that we confiscated from the Feds since they're bullet proof. Be sure to bring a SAW with a lot of ammo and some grenades."

I pulled a map out to determine what would be the best route to take. There are two routes we could take. One way we pass through somewhat safe neighborhoods by driving down Gulf Blvd. to

Pasadena Ave. which turns into 66th Street.

The other route is taking 34th Street to 1st Ave. North. Then take that to 66th Street. Once on 66th Street it is a straight shot to Albert's home located on 30th Ave. North.

The problem is we haven't been that far north using either route. We really don't have any idea if either is safe. If Sgt. Cain, the Drone Master, was here I could have a Drone fly the routes to check them out before we leave. But that's not possible. One thing I didn't like was we would have to go past the Mall which could be packed with all kinds of weird people.

I made my mind up to take Gulf Blvd. to 66th Street. We would travel 100 yards apart. If one truck gets attacked it can withdraw quickly. The other vehicle will be the backup. We would take the two black SUVs which we picked up a while back from the Feds at Ellenton because they are bullet proof and have run flat tires.

Amy will be with Tommy in one and Maggie will be in the other with me and Albert. I'll drive and take the lead. It was ten am as we pulled off of Tocabaga and our family waved good bye to us. The women weren't happy we were leaving but didn't make any verbal objections.

As we drove down Gulf Blvd. we saw a few

people walking around but not many. It was an eerie sight watching people roaming around like zombies searching for food. Some tried to wave us down and yelled for us to stop. A few people had guns but no one shot at us. We proceeded past the dilapidated Pasadena Hospital where we saw a few cars driving around and wondered what they were doing.

Hospitals use to be a safe place to go if you became sick. After the government took control of everything they became a place of death. If you were old and went there for an operation or illness you never came out alive. People just stopped going to the hospitals because it was too risky. Most of them have been closed over the years. Small clinics owned by real Doctors, operating under the radar without government approval, are where most people go now for medical care.

Driving the lead truck I had just turned the bend from Pasadena Ave. onto 66th Street losing sight of the other vehicle as we went around the sharp curve in the road. I looked in my mirror and saw a car coming up fast from behind and … BAM … it rammed us in the back end jarring the whole truck.

Maggie yelled, "What the fuck is that guy doing?"

Maggie got on the radio to Amy, "We're under attack!"

BAM ... it rammed us gain so I hit the gas.

Amy replied, "Ok, we'll be right there."

I told Maggie and Albert, "Get your guns ready he's pulling up on the passenger side. We can't outrun them. When he's next to us I'll slam on the brakes and stop, then we'll jump out and start shooting."

The car pulled up next to us at 60 mph. We observed there were four men inside and three of them were aiming handguns at us. I slammed on the brakes coming to a tire-screeching stop and the car went zooming past us, just as I planned. They slammed on their brakes and started to back up from about 200 feet away.

The three of us jumped out of the truck and started to fire our M4s' on full auto peppering the back of the car. One of our bullets hit their gas tank and the car burst into flames but it was still slowly rolling towards us.

I yelled, "Maggie, Albert, get inside." Climbing back in I mashed the gas to pull away just as the men in the other car were jumping out. I pulled forward about 200 feet and stopped again. We dismounted and started shooting at the fools.

Our other truck sped onto 66th Street with Amy standing in the sun roof firing the SAW light machine gun. I watched four men fall to the ground riddled with bullets and then … KABOOM … the gas tank blew creating a huge fire ball. The whole incident was over in about five minutes.

Tommy pulled up next to our truck and I told them, "Good job!"

Amy replied, "No problem Daddy O. That'll teach them. You don't mess with the Gunn family!" That's what; I like family loyalty.

We were approaching the Mall area and I got on the radio, "Tommy, speed it up to about sixty miles per hour to zoom by the mall. I don't want to have any problems here."

"Roger that," he replied.

Speeding by the mall I glanced out my window to see the poor homeless people wandering around the mall parking lot. It looked just like the scene at Ellenton. I didn't want to go there because the people at this mall are of a different character. They are meaner and more violent than the simple country folk at Ellenton.

Years ago, when things were going downhill and before Tocabaga came into existence, I went to the mall to purchase some boots. I was at the main entrance and noticed an old woman rummaging in the garbage can for food. She had a babushka on her head and wore an old black heavy wool coat even though it was 90 degrees outside. My Grandmother used to wear a babushka so she reminded me of her. I walked up to her and said, "Grandmother, here take this and buy something to eat," as I handed her one hundred dollars.

She replied, "Danke sehr," which is German for thank you. She couldn't speak English and it surprised me because my Grandmother was also German. I gently took her old wrinkled hand putting the money in it and she cried. I led her to the food court and purchased a cup of soup and a sandwich for her. Then I went to the security office and told the officer about her. He advised me she comes around every Tuesday at noon. I asked him to watch out for her when she comes around.

I would go to the mall each Tuesday at noon and give Grandma a hundred bucks. After about six months Grandma didn't show up. No one knew what happened to her, she just disappeared. I should have done more to help her. My guess is some dirtbag killed her for the money I gave her. Weird shady people hang around at the mall looking for easy prey like old helpless women. That's why I don't like the mall. People think there's safety in hanging around in a large group. That's only true if they are honest people of good character.

As we approached 30ᵗʰ Ave. I started to slow down because I noticed there was a road block with four men standing guard making it impossible to proceed. I stopped about 100 feet away and Albert said, "Wait here. I know these guys. Let me go talk to them." Our backup vehicle stopped behind us as Albert got out leaving his M4 behind and approached the men.

Albert yelled to them, "Hey guys it's me, Albert Madison." They waved him over to the road block.

Tommy and Amy got out and came over to my truck and we discussed the situation. I said, "It looks like we're not going to be able to take the trucks down 29th. If Albert goes in two of us will go with him and the others stay here guarding the SUVs. I suggest Maggie and I go in with Albert."

Maggie replied, "Ok, sounds good to me."

"If we get in trouble, Tommy, you ram though the road block and pick us up. Amy, you provide cover fire for the group. Everyone got it?" All replied we got it.

I wanted Maggie to go with me because she had already been tested in combat and has 3 kills to her name. She wouldn't hesitate to kill someone who was a threat. Maggie recently killed Scotty and

Farmer Horn, shooting him in the eye when he tried to kidnap her for breeding purposes.

I was watching Albert talk to the four men. They pointed at us and it seemed they were discussing who we were. Ten minutes later Albert walked back to us advising, "They'll let us in so I can talk to my wife, Sue. The bad news is my son is dead and she is living with another guy named Buck who is the head man on this block. My friends told me he runs everything and they're afraid of him because he's in a motorcycle gang. He has six gang members with him at all times."

I said, "Sorry to hear about your son, Albert. How did he die?"

"They didn't say, so I don't know."

I asked Albert, "How many men live here?"

"I don't know how many now but there used to be fifteen men who lived on this block. However there's one problem."

"What's the problem?"

"We can't take any guns in with us."

"Shit … that's a big problem. I should have known that would happen."

"They did promise me we would be safe."

"Yep, I've heard that before. Well I guess if you want to see your wife we better get going. Maggie hide your subcompact Glock in your panties and keep your machete on. They won't frisk you there but they'll search me."

"Tommy, I'll have my radio to stay in touch. If I say the words FUBAR bust down the road block with the SUV and you guys come to the rescue in one truck. Amy shoot everybody and everything with that machine gun."

Amy replied, "I think it's too risky. It would be better if Albert went in by himself and if he gets into trouble then we can all come to his rescue."

I thought about this for a minute and Tommy spoke up, "Dad, Amy is right. Albert should go by himself and if he gets into trouble then we'll have four guns to save him."

I looked at Albert and asked him, "Well Al, what do you think?"

"I think they're right but I don't think I can handle it by myself. I know the men at this road block are big chicken shits and if shooting starts they'll run for the hills. The problem is I don't know Buck and his men. It could get nasty real quick."

"I don't like letting Albert go in by himself so let's stick with my original plan. If Albert goes by himself it makes him look weak so they might take advantage of it and kill him on the spot."

I would try to bring in my Black Bear knife for use as a possible weapon. Maggie had a gun shoved in her panties and the machete hanging from her belt so we had some weapons if needed.

We walked over to the guards and they frisked Albert and me but didn't say a word about my fighting knife. They went to frisk Maggie and she yelled at them, "You touch me and it'll be the last thing you ever touch," as she put her hand on the big machete. They let her pass with no further comments.

We walked down the middle of the street with Albert in the lead. I tried to observe every detail I could. Taking in my surroundings, making a mental note of everything, who was on the street, how many people there were, and who had guns with them. For the most part there were only a few people outside due to the heat. It was noon and here in Florida people don't stand around outside in the 98 degree heat. They find some shade to sit in and hope for a cool breeze.

After walking about a quarter mile Albert said, "Here's my house." We walked up four steps to a small porch and he knocked on the screen door.

A woman came to the door and said, "Oh

my God, it's you Albert." She started to cry. Albert's wife, Sue, was about 45 years old and in her younger days she was probably a beautiful woman. Now she looked old and worn out.

She opened the screen door stepping out into the sunlight and you could see bruises on her face and arms. It looked like her nose was broken and her teeth were rotten. You could tell she had been beaten by someone. Al wrapped her in his arms and hugged her for a few minutes as he wept.

The screen door opened again and out stepped an ugly-looking guy who said in a deep voice, "Hey! She's my bitch. Who the hell are you?"

I saw the gun right away, it was a big Desert Eagle pistol, in a shoulder holster under his left arm. He had his hand on the grip, getting ready to draw, as he visually checked us out to see if we had any guns. Satisfied we didn't he lowered his right arm which was covered in tattoos.

Albert replied, "I'm Albert her husband."

"I'm Buck the Boss man around here and I told you she's my bitch now."

I looked at Maggie and she had her hand on the machete. Buck looked at me and asked, "Who the hell are you guys?"

"I'm Jack Gunn and this is Maggie. We're here to help Albert."

"You're here to help Albert do what?"

"We're here to help him get back his wife." Buck laughed at that comment and roughly pulled Albert's wife over to him.

I was surprised that Albert didn't object more strongly because he only said, "Don't do that."

Buck replied, "What are you going to do about it geek. I should kill all three of you right now," as he stepped up to Albert's face. Albert immediately backed away from him not wanting to escalate the confrontation. Buck is a bully and I hate all bullies so in my mind this guy needed to die.

Buck was about 50 years old and about 6 feet tall. He looked like a big slob but I'm sure he was strong. He had a long gray beard covering his face. A bandana was wrapped around his fat head keeping his long black hair tied back and he wore a black leather vest which showed his motorcycle gang colors. The tattoos on his arms and neck showed he was into white supremacy. He was the gang leader and cycle gangs' deal in selling meth and other drugs. Maybe that's why Sue's teeth were rotten. I wondered how many gang members we would run into.

Buck smiled, an evil smile, while looking at Maggie and said, "Ok, Albert can have this old bitch back and I'll take this pretty little thing." He pushed Sue back into Albert's arms.

Buck is a bully and bullies usually get their way by intimidation and threats. They like to make their prey suffer and beg. Bullies are really cowards and only fight if they know they can win. He has no idea what he is up against.

"Maggie, I like that army outfit you got on. It's kind of kinky. How come you got that on?"

"I wear this because I'm a Warrior, an Amazon Warrior."

"A warrior uh, well warrior on this," and he grabbed his crotch.

"Come over here little warrior girl." Buck reached over to grab Maggie's arm and she quickly pulled back while drawing out the Barong.

Maggie replied, "You touch me asshole and I'll cut your fucking arm off."

I put my hand on the Black Bear getting ready to draw it out. I never draw my knife unless I'm going to slice someone. I guessed that I could draw my Cold Steel Black Bear fighting knife and stab him in the throat before he could get that cannon out of its shoulder holster. I probably could kill him three times before he drew that big gun. So right now we had the advantage with him standing so close to us. He had no idea what we could do to him in a split second.

It occurred to me that Buck was the only person here. Where are the others? Are they sleeping or drugged up … if so then this is the time to kill Buck and take Albert's wife back.

Buck spoke softly in a low growl warning Maggie, "Look you little bitch, put that thing away or I'm going to take it and hurt you real bad. You ain't got the guts to use that pigsticker."

I knew what was going to happen next because I knew Maggie. Stupid Buck didn't have any idea what he was getting into. He was going to activate a killing machine.

He reached out his right arm and grabbed for Maggie again so I knew what was coming … WHACK. I heard the blade strike the bone in his right arm at the wrist, which was his gun hand, chopping it off slick as a whistle.

He watched his hand fall to the floor making a plopping noise when it landed. Blood was squirting in pulses out of his arm as Buck tried to stop the profuse bleeding.

I yelled FUBAR into the radio signaling Tommy to come pick us up. Maggie reached deep into her panties pulling out the little Glock 26 and tossed it to me. I racked a round into the chamber. I was going to shoot Buck, but didn't because it would have made too much noise.

Buck was crying like a baby while holding his bloody arm, "My hand, you cut off my fucking hand." He fell to his knees in shock and tried to reattach the severed hand to the bloody stump.

I shouted, "Maggie finish him off!"

Maggie grabbed him by the hair and said, "Ok, don't move Buck or this could hurt. Wait for it … wait for it!"

Buck was on his knees in shock and couldn't move or speak. He just gazed at Maggie with his eyes wide open as she pulled him by the hair, holding his head up high, to expose his throat.

Maggie took another powerful swing … WHACK … cutting off his head. Actually his head was dangling by the spinal cord. It was kind of swinging in the air like a bobble head doll as he fell over dead on the blood splattered floor.

Maggie said with a frown on her face, "Fuck you, Buck! I told you not to touch me!"

I told Albert, his wife, and Maggie to run for it. I covered the door as they made their escape. I was standing next to the door, back up against the wall, when four dudes came running out to see what was causing all the commotion. They saw Buck laying there headless and were startled. The dopes didn't see me standing behind them as they gazed at Buck's bloody body.

One dumb dork yelled, "Holy shit, who the fuck did this?"

I greeted them, "Howdy boys. It's time to meet your maker."

As they turned around to see who was speaking I shot each one in the head, from six feet away, in rapid order ... BAM ... BAM ... BAM ... BAM ... they dropped to the ground one after the other like bowling pins. I couldn't miss at that range.

A head shot will kill a person almost every time, but a great head shot right between the eyes makes a person just drop to the floor like a bag of beans leaving no doubt they are dead. It takes a lot of practice to make a great head shot.

I jumped off the porch and made a run for it. I heard machine gun fire coming from the road block meaning Amy had killed the four men guarding it. The black SUV came crashing thru the cars blocking the way. Tommy stopped, picking up Maggie, Albert, and Sue. By the time they were all in the truck I arrived and jumped in right behind them. I yelled, "Let's get the hell out of here."

Tommy backed up crashing through the road block in reverse. He stopped next to our other truck so Maggie and I scooted out, and quickly climbed into it. I cranked up the motor and we sped away at full speed following Tommy.

Speeding by the Mall Maggie said, "That was easy!"

"Maggie, you're one crazy bitch but I really mean that in a nice way. Your timing was perfect when you sliced that jerk up. It was a thing of beauty. I knew you would cut off his arm when he tried to touch you."

Maggie looked at me and smiled while letting out a little giggle, "Thanks Jack, that means a lot to me and I knew you had my back. We make a good team."

"In just one swing of the Barong you cut off his fucking head. I liked it when you told him … don't move Buck or this could hurt. That was really funny!"

We both started to laugh to ease our tensions and reduce the adrenaline that was flowing through our bodies. My hands were trembling as I was driving so I lit up a smoke to relax me.

I looked at Maggie, who sat there with a

smile on her face and commented, "We're lucky we won this fight. You can tell the story at the fire circle tonight."

"It wasn't luck, it was skill." Maggie had a lot of confidence in herself, maybe too much confidence.

"Yes, your skill killed Buck, but we were lucky today."

"Oh shut up, Jack, and give me my gun back before you sniff the grip." We laughed as I pulled the gun from my belt and smelled the pistol grip that had been sitting between her legs deep inside her panties.

"Jack, you're a dirty old man but you're the best friend I have," as she grabbed the gun from my hand.

"Maggie, don't put that back in your panties. People will think you're weird using a gun as a dildo."

"Jack, I am weird. What else would I use for a dildo? The gun turns me on."

That comment cracked us both up and we laughed all the way back to Tocabaga. I thought if Robbie, Maggie's husband and my best friend, was still alive he'd be laughing also and he'd be damn proud of her. Maggie and I never talk about Robbie because it's too painful. His death is buried deep in our memories.

We arrived back on Tocabaga with no further attacks or incidents. As we dismounted from the truck Albert and his wife came over to us. We shook hands as Albert thanked Maggie and me for saving his wife. Sue hugged both of us and started cry when she saw her kids running down the road to meet her.

Sue ran to them holding out her arms and scooped them up in a big hug. It was a heartwarming moment. Albert standing told us, "I can never thank you both enough for saving my wife and killing Buck. I owe you guys big time."

I said, "Albert, you owe us nothing. That's what we're all about, helping each other, fighting for each other, saving each other, and if needed killing the bad guys who want to do us harm."

"Sue told me Buck moved into our house and took control of her and forced Ed out. They got into a fight so Buck just pulled out his gun and shot Ed in cold blood right in front of Sue. Thanks to you guys I got to witness justice first hand. Seeing Buck get his just due enables us to move on with our lives. Thank you so much."

We hugged each other and then Albert trotted over to his wife and kids. I told Maggie, "I gotta check on the newbies over in the High & Dry."

Maggie said, "I need to check what's going on at the farm. See you later, Jack." As I watched her walk away I thanked God for watching over us. Maggie was right. It wasn't luck, it was God, skill, and good timing that helped us return safely.

Albert took his wife to see Doc Scott for a checkup. He found she was addicted to meth so she would have to kick that bad habit. They could pull some of her bad teeth but to replace missing ones was another big problem. Maybe the SOCOM clinic could help her.

I walked over to my house and the kids were outside playing baseball. They wanted me to play but I told them maybe later and I went inside for a warm beer. Warm or not it still tasted good. My wife walked in the kitchen and I gave her a kiss on the cheek. She asked, "So you found Albert's wife ok?"

"Yep we found her. Sue is going to be ok but we found out that Albert's son Ed was killed by a guy named Buck who was living in her house. So to make a long story short Maggie killed him and we escaped with Sue."

Hemmi asked me, "Did you have to kill anyone?"

"Of course I did. You know I hate bullies and gangs. Have you seen Ron or Jim Bo?"

"I think they're guarding the new people at the High and Dry."

"Ok, I gotta go see what's going on over there. I'll be back soon."

I didn't want to tell my wife the whole gory story how Maggie killed Buck and how I shot four gang members. She doesn't need to know the details. I guess I'm too protective.

I walked over to the High & Dry and found my brother Ron standing in the doorway and asked him, "Hey Bro, what's going on? Anybody get cleared yet?"

"Hi Bro, yep a few have been cleared. I see you brought back Albert's wife. How did that go?"

"Really good, none of us got hurt and we terminated five gang members."

"Jack, there's something strange going on. You know that Stan Gill ... well they ran him through the system and there is no Stan Gill. No record of Stan Gill at all."

"No record at all? Are they sure?"

"Yep positive, they checked his prints and photo, but this guy does not exist. He's not in the system and is totally off the grid."

"Well that could mean he's a spy for someone or he's an undercover operator or somehow managed to not be processed. It's impossible not to be in the system. Where is Gill at now? We need to ask him some questions."

"I asked everyone during the interview if they ever saw Stan at the Dome. No one saw him at the Dome. They don't know where he came from, so we've been keeping a close eye on him."

Jim Bo came over to us and advised, "Hey, you guys, Stan Gill is missing. Have you seen him?"

I ran into the building with Ron behind me. I told Ron, "Do a head count and see how many are missing. Jim Bo, help Ron out and then post pictures of those that are missing all over Tocabaga. We need to double the guard here."

Ron and Jim counted heads and found two people were missing. Stan Gill and Ken Johnson were nowhere to be found. The funny thing is Johnson's background checked out ok except he was an ex-felon. He spent six years in prison for grand theft.

Jim Bo had their pictures printed and handed them out to our security teams. In addition, they were posted on every light pole on the island. It would be dark soon so I wanted to find these guys fast. I wondered what they're up too.

I went home to have dinner with the family while Tommy and the rest of my crew searched the island. They would shoot these men on sight. There was no place they could hide. I had 120 people searching for them, looking in every corner, every car, every boat, and every house.

I opened the back door to my house and heard Johnny yell, "Watch out, Grandpa, bad guys are here!" I drew my Glock without saying a word and slowly crept up the stairs into the living room.

Standing there was Stan and Ken with guns pointed at my family. Stan said, "Don't move, Jack. Drop your guns now or we'll shoot your whole family."

I dropped my guns to the floor and replied, "Ok, let them go now."

"We're not stupid, Jack, we can't let them go just yet." They rounded everyone up, except for Johnny, and shoved them into the half bathroom. They pushed a chair under the door handle so they couldn't get out. Stan held the gun on little Johnny while keeping an eye on me. Ken walked over to me, picked up my guns and took my Black Bear knife.

Ken told me, "Turn around." I turned around and he tied my hands behind my back.

I asked, "Who are you guys and what do you want?"

Stan answered, "I thought that would be obvious. We want you, Jack Gunn, for the murder of eight Federal Agents at Ellenton. We're U.S. Deputy Marshals and you're under arrest."

"If you're Marshals, then show me your badges."

"We don't need no stinking badges!"

"I didn't kill those Agents, the mob at Ellenton did it."

"You're responsible because you took their guns and vehicles. One of those men was my brother. We're going to make an example of you. Your execution will be on TV for everyone to see so you'll be a star. I'll take a video of it so I can watch you die over and over again."

Ken pushed me down the stairs with the barrel of his gun saying, "Ok, get going Jack," while Stan held on to Johnny.

I said, "Let the kid go. He didn't do anything."

Stan replied, "He's coming along for insurance so you don't try anything stupid."

As we walked out the door I commented, "You'll never get away. You'll never get off of

Tocabaga."

"Yes we will or the kid and you both die. You'll get us by the roadblock. Now get in the SUV. This is the one you stole from us." The black SUV was parked just outside my home. It was the same one we just used to rescue Sue. I knew something they didn't know about the SUV.

Ken was driving as we pulled up to the bridge. I was in the back seat with Stan and Johnny. Stan told Johnny, "Don't say a word kid or I'll kill your Grandpa."

I yelled out the window, "Chris, move the road block I'm going out." It wasn't Chris it was Tony. I was trying to tip them off.

Suddenly Tommy came running up to the truck and asked, "Hey Dad, where are you going?" He looked in the SUV and saw Stan so he immediately pointed his M4 at him.

Stan shouted, "Stand down or I shoot Jack and Johnny. I'm a US Marshal and Jack is under arrest for murder."

I told Tommy, "Put the gun down. He's got the drop on us. Open the road block," as I gave him a wink.

"You'll never get away with this," Tommy told Stan.

The road block was moved and 30 minutes later Ken sped over the bridge taking us off Tocabaga as my men stood there watching. I asked Stan, "Where are we going?"

"We're going to Atlanta where you will be put on trial and then shot by a firing squad. I'll be on that squad."

"What about Johnny? What are you going to do with him?"

"We'll let him go in a few miles when we're sure no one is following us."

Ken drove the truck up the entrance ramp to Interstate 275 heading north toward Tampa. The one thing these bright boys didn't take into account was the gas. The gas tank was almost empty and in a few miles it'll run dry. Maybe I can escape with Johnny when that happens. I also knew that Tommy and my best shooters would be coming after us.

We were about a half mile from the 54th Ave. exit when the motor sputtered and we rolled to a stop on the side of the highway. Stan asked, "What's wrong?"

Ken commented, "Shit! We're out of gas."

"You dumb ass. Why didn't you check it? Get your butt out and go find some gas or get another car. Hurry up we'll wait here!"

I knew Ken had a long walk ahead of him. I watched him walk north toward 54th Ave. at a fast pace until he disappeared into the darkness. I checked the time; it was 9:30 pm.

I asked Stan, "Who are the other people that came to Tocabaga with you?"

Stan replied with a smirk on his face, "Wouldn't you like to know."

"Ya, I would like to know. I'm going to be dead so it doesn't matter."

"Ok, I'll tell you. Some of them were real prisoners from the Dome but most of them are undercover Federal agents who are going to take over Tocabaga and get your group in line. We're going to turn it into a green zone and boot out the Army. The plans have been made and Federal Police Troops will be arriving there in a few days."

I thought, what a stupid shit. He just told the whole plan in front of Johnny who will warn Tommy if Stan lets him go.

"You know Stan, the FPF already attempted to take over Tocabaga but that failed and a lot of them were killed."

"That was only because you had the Rangers there. They won't be there this time to save your butts. I planned this whole thing. You're so easy to fool.

"What the hell happen to Ken, he's been gone two hours?"

I was thinking, I gotta get out of this mess and warn everyone of the pending attack. We were sitting there for two hours waiting for Ken to return with more gas when Johnny said, "I gotta pee."

Stan opened the truck door got out and said, "Ok, kid, go pee over there in the grass." Johnny got out and took a few steps to the grass and Stan was standing near him when I heard it.

A bullet whizzed by Stan and then another. One hit him in the torso knocking him to the ground. I shouted to Johnny, "Quick come here and untie me!"

Johnny jumped in the truck and untied my hands. I jumped out and grabbed Stan's handgun, which happened to be one of my Glocks. I checked his pulse, he was dead. I jumped back into the bullet-proof SUV and wondered who shot Stan.

Tommy never misses, his motto is one shot one kill. I concluded the shooter couldn't have been Tommy because he doesn't miss. I wondered who shot Stan.

I locked all the doors as Johnny peered out the windows looking for the shooter. Johnny said,

"Look, Grandpa, some people are coming this way."

Looking out the windshield I saw them, a group of people, coming towards us out of the darkness. The people were too far away to make out who they were. I could only see dark shadow-like figures walking slowly in our direction.

I turned around looking out the back window and there were more people coming from behind us. I thought to myself oh no FUBAR! Are these gang people, Federal Police, or who?

Johnny asked, "What do we do now, Grandpa?"

"Don't worry, Johnny, they can't get in this bullet proof truck. You just keep your head down and Grandpa will take care of it. I want you to sit on the floor." Grandpa was very worried to say the least.

I rolled up all the windows and made sure the doors were locked. I pulled down the inside sun shades to cover the windows so they couldn't see who was inside the truck. I smashed the interior lights so I could open the door if needed without lighting up the interior of the truck thereby making us easy targets.

I said a silent prayer, "God do what you will with me, but please protect little Johnny from evil."

I checked my gun and made sure there was a round in the chamber and waited as they approached. I only had 17 rounds and no extra ammunition. I looked again and both groups where within 200 yards. They were slowly closing in on us one step at a time.

I'm burned out and need some rest. I'll write some more later right now I need a shot of JD, but you won't believe what happens next.

It never ends, why can't the Feds leave us alone? Why can't we live in peace? Why do they have to control everything and everybody?

I know one thing I will never give up and neither will the good citizens of Tocabaga.

That's all for now.

GOD BLESS AMERICA, LAND OF THE FREE, AND HOME OF THE BRAVE!

Jack Gunn

PS: Read my article below on Gun Selection It gives advice to first time gun buyers … how to choose the correct gun for defense or hunting.

GUN SELECTION

This article will cover gun selection based on what is the most popular ammunition. The gun is your most important asset. Without ammunition, however, your gun is worthless. What kind of guns should one own? Based on my 40 years of gun experience the type of gun and caliber is very important for your protection. Guns have only two main purposes which are hunting and self protection. Of course, any of the guns mentioned in this article can be used for hunting as well as self defense. The question is which gun is the best tool for the job.

For people new to guns I try to explain the differences in a simple manner. When purchasing your first gun it is a confusing matter to choose the correct gun with the large selection in the market. I have had many people ask me, what type of gun should I purchase? Where do you go to learn to shoot?

GUNS FOR HUNTING

The most popular ammunition is the .22 long round and the 12 gauge shotgun round. This ammo is easy to obtain and that is what is important. The more popular the ammo is the easier it is to find when you run out of ammunition.

I break down guns into two categories which are hunting guns and tactical guns or combat weapons. There may come a time when you will need to hunt for food. There are two types of hunting guns that can dispatch most animals and that is a 12 gauge shotgun and a .22 caliber rifle or pistol. These two guns allow you good flexibility. The shotgun you can use bird shot for hunting birds or rabbits and slugs for hunting deer or larger animals. In addition a 12 gauge with slugs or buck shot is a great weapon to use for protection at close range.

The one drawback is that shotgun shells are expensive and heavy to carry and too large to store many of them. Shotguns come mostly in semi-automatic and pump type. They hold 5 to 8 rounds. The difference is the semi-auto you just load and pull the trigger. The faster you pull the trigger the faster it shoots. The pump needs to be pumped or cocked each time to shoot it. I prefer the semi-auto type because it is faster, easier to clean and use. Double barrel or single shot shotguns are not worth owning since you have to reload every time you fire it.

Do not under estimate the .22 rifle or long barrel pistol as it can be used on birds and or small rodents as well as be a tool for self defense. A .22 with hollow point bullets is an easy weapon to use and you can carry a lot of ammunition since the bullets are so small. You can store 5,000 rounds of this ammo in a desk due to its small size. A .22 rifle has a 200 yard range and 6 inch barrel pistol has a 50 yard range.

The 12 gauge shotgun and a .22caliber rifle are a must to own. A .22 rifle also comes in pump or semi-auto types. The choice is up to you. As for 22 pistols there is only one that I will mention and that is the Ruger target model as it is the best you can buy.

My selection for a shotgun is a Remington semi-auto model that handles 2 ¾ inch shells. Purchase a shotgun that has a stock and forearm that is made of modern plastic as it can stand up better to the elements.

GUNS FOR SELF DEFENSE

There are many types of combat pistol and rifle ammunition. The selection of the ammunition is critical to the type of combat rifle or combat pistol you will select for protection. The shotgun and .22 rifle mentioned above are dual purpose weapons but are mainly for hunting. The pistols and rifles mentioned below are really the weapons you need for total protection. These are guns that contain high capacity magazines.

What other types of guns do you need to survive? Well let us first look at what is the most popular type of ammunition used to make our selection. Having enough ammo will be your biggest problem. The fact is most police and military handguns are 9 mm. The 45 caliber and 40 calibers are also popular but not as common as 9mm luger ammo. The 9mm ammo is also less expensive to purchase.

For rifles there are only three major types of calibers that are widely used by the police and military. One is the .223 Winchester also known as the 5.56mm NATO round. The other is the AK 47 round 7.62 x39, a round used by the military and some police around the world. This is the most popular ammo used by terrorists and gangs because the AK 47 is an inexpensive weapon or rifle. The last is the .308 Winchester round or 7.62x51 NATO.

The .223 ammo is used by the famous Colt AR15 or the M16 which is now named the M4 carbine, widely used by our military. There are many different manufactures of the so called AR15 design. Some of these AR designs also shoot 7.62x51 NATO which is the basically the same as the .308 Winchester and are called AR10 rifles.

The 7.62x39 and 7.62x51 are not to be confused as they are totally different rounds. The drawback of the 7.62x51round is the cost is higher than the .223 and when you are hauling around 300 rounds they are also heavier. The 7.62 x 51 is a long range round and can exceed 800 yards. The .223 round has an effective range of up to 500 yards.

You can also purchase an AR type rifle that will fire the AK 47 7.62x39mm round. Bushmaster is one of the best manufactures for AR type designs which can be purchased in many different calibers. Several companies also make a .22 caliber AR rifle such as Colt and the Smith and Wesson M&P 15-22.

The most popular type ammunition for a pistol is the 9mm luger round. The most common type for a rifle is the .223 Winchester, also known as the 5.56mmNATO round. Knowing this we can select a number of different pistols, rifles, or carbines to use. For this selection we need to keep in mind durability, ease of cleaning, interchangeability, and ease of use by men or women.

Knowing that we want a handgun that shoots 9mm luger rounds you can note that all 9mm are semi-auto design and are not revolvers. Semi-auto means it has a magazine that holds the bullets and some can hold up to 18 rounds before reloading. There are two handguns that I recommend which are a

Glock and a Springfield Armory model XD. I own both and they are the best dependable handguns on the market. This is not to say there are not other good brands but based on my shooting experience buying one of these handguns you cannot go wrong.

My favorite is the Glock Model 17 because it is dependable and very easy to clean and repair. Yes, sometimes guns break so you should have some extra parts or a backup gun or two if possible. Each gun comes with an assembly manual and the Glock can be taken apart by just removing the slide and one pin which is pushed out. I have shot thousands of rounds and only had my Glock break one time. The trigger return spring broke and I replaced it in 10 minutes with a new one. It is so simple that anyone can work on it. The Glock can be dropped in the mud, run over by a truck and still shoot. It can be fired under water and the barrel life is 350,000 rounds which is more than you will ever shoot in your life time.

Basically all AR15 type rifles are the same design and are easy to take apart for cleaning. The models may have different names from different manufactures such as Armalite SPR Mod 1 which is basically the same as a Colt CAR15 or carbine model of the AR 15 rifle.

It pays to buy a good quality rifle from a well known manufacturer even if it may cost a little more. Remember your life may depend on this weapon. If you buy an AR type rifle then find out what parts you may need to replace by asking the manufacture. I recommend buying two weapons of the same type this way you have a back up and you do not have to learn about different weapons and the assemblies. Parts between different manufactures' are not necessarily interchangeable. The AR15 can be cleaned in about 10 minutes just by pushing out a pin which opens the rifle up. It is also light weight so men and women can use it. The recoil is very low which is important for accurate firing. I recommend the Colt brand AR15 .223 as this is a dependable weapon which has been on the market many years.

Some manufactures such as Colt have also made CAR15 carbines that use the pistol 9mm luger round. This is an excellent weapon that has very little recoil but has a limited range of about 100 yards. It is made for close quarter combat situations. Having a CAR15 9mm is a good choice since you can use the same ammo as your 9mm handgun.

To summarize the guns needed are; a 12 gauge shotgun semi-automatic type, a .22 rifle or target pistol, a 9mm luger Glock handgun, and a .223 (5.56 NATO) AR15 design rifle or a CAR15 9mm carbine. I would choose to have two guns of each type so you have a backup. How much ammo do you need? It is up to you to decide, but the more the better as the gun is worthless without ammunition. If you can only own one or two guns then the AR15 rifle and the 9mm Glock are my choices.

Everyone in your family should know how to shoot each type of gun. I suggest one gun for each family member. Gun selection should be made by what each member of the family likes best to shoot. One may like a .22 caliber and one may like a 9mm Glock. Remember your family is also your Army to help protect each other. So proper training is very important. Do not spare any expense on training. Do not buy cheap unreliable guns.

GUN SAFETY

If you have no experience with guns then it is suggested that you learn by going to your local gun store or shooting range and take lessons from a good instructor. If you have a friend who shoots go with him to the range. The National Rifle Association or NRA is a valuable resource to use for this learning process.

NRA has safety rules which you can find listed on line. The worst thing you can do is buy a gun and not know how to use it or even load it. If you are faced with a threat to your life or that of your family then you better know how to use the weapon with some degree of skill. The more skillful you are the better your chance of survival will be. We are talking life and death situations that require split second decisions on your part so shooting practice is a very necessary. Join a local shooting club.

I stress do not buy a gun just to have one. Do not buy a gun if you will never practice or shoot it. How much practice do you need? Based on my experience I think shooting your weapon at least one to two hours per week is necessary to become a good shot and learn to know everything about your gun. I know many people who shoot two hours a week. I also stress go take combat shooting lessons at a gun school such as Gun Sight or Front Sight. They will train you in Home Defense, Vehicle Defense, Tactical Rifle, Pistol, and Shotgun use. Be the best you can be as learning to shoot is more than just going to the range and pulling the trigger.

Above all be a safe shooter and follow the safety rules. When not in use keep you guns locked up so kids cannot access them and they cannot be stolen from you. I strongly suggest a gun safe to store your guns and ammo as it will give you peace of mind. You can also keep other valuables in the safe. Shooting can be a great hobby providing much enjoyment and fun for the whole family. Shoot safe and shoot straight.

DRAMATIS PERSONAE

Albert Madison – Navy Vet. who comes to Tocabaga with wife and two kids

Barry – A quisling killed by the Gunn family

Billy – Kid found living on the street with his sister Rosie and brother Peter

Bok Lam – A Chinese man and close friend of Jack's since high school

Buck – Motorcycle gang leader killed by Maggie

Chase – A quisling

Colonel Turner – Commanding Officer of the Army Rangers based at Fort Desoto

Corporal Phillips – In charge of the communications office at Fort Desoto

Captain Sessions – Combat officer, commands and controls combat operations in the field

Captain Riley – Female tank commander, girl friend of Captain Sessions

Chris – Tocabaga security guard and close friend of Jack

Dew – A quisling killed by the Gunn family

Dr. Carl Urban – The inventor of the RCCD Units

and friend of Jack's

Dr. Carl Urban, Jr. – Son of Dr. Urban

Dr. Alvin Sinclair – Robot inventor and Commie killed by Jack

Ellen – A lonely woman

First Lt. Fisher – TALOS Warrior, Platoon commander

Farmer John – An old farmer saved by Jack, now living on Tocabaga

Guy Allen or GA – Suspected spy living on Tocabaga was killed by Jack

General Harper – Commander of the Rangers located at SOCOM

George Taylor – A nice kid who was bullied in school by Nick

Hemmi – Wife of Jack Gunn

Joe – RCCD tech. Supervisor; a tough guy killed by Jack

Little Johnny – Adopted grandson of Jack's

Johnny the Fisherman – A quisling killed by security

Jill – A warrior killed by Feds

Jim Bo – Husband to Amy and son-in-law of Jack

Jimmy Smith – A bully from years ago

Ken – US Deputy Marshal who went missing

Leroy – The man who killed Jack's little brother Mike

Mike – Jack Gunn's little brother killed by a doper

Maggie – Wife of Robbie, who is in charge of the farming

Mr. Johnson or Famer John – Old time Farmer

Mr. Horn – Pig farmer and dirtbag who wanted to kidnap Maggie for breeding

Nick – A bully from Junior High School

Peter – Little nine year old brother to Rosie

Rosie – A fifteen year old girl Jack found living on the street

Robbie – Best friend of Jack Gunn, a Tocabaga security guard killed by the FPF on April 27, 2025

Ron – Brother of Jack Gunn Retired Navy vet. Part of Tocabaga security.

Rick – President of Tocabaga Association, security team member

Sally – A warrior killed by Feds

Scotty – A quisling killed by security

Sergeant Hammer – Army Ranger

Sergeant First Class Dale – killed in action

Sergeant Major Willis – Ranger squad leader and security guard for Jack

Sergeant Cain – the Drone Master

Sergeant Smith - Army Ranger assigned as security guard for Jack

Stan – Deputy Marshal

Sue – Wife of Albert Madison

Tommy Gunn – Son of Jack Gunn and a retired Marine Scout Sniper

Tony – Bar keeper and sharp-shooter for Tocabaga security

Trini – Amazon Warrior who killed Troy

Troy – A quisling killed by security

Victor Elway – An old farmer from Ellenton now living on Tocabaga with his friend Farmer John

Zack – A quisling killed by the Gunn family

OTHER BOOKS BY THOMAS H. WARD

THE TOCABAGA CHRONICLES:

TOCABAGA 1: Revised Edition

TOCABAGA 2: Theoterrorism

TOCABAGA 3: Warm Blood – Cold Steel

TOCABAGA 4: The Talos Warriors

TOCABAGA 5: The Quislings & Androktones

TOCABAGA 6: The Dimachaerus Clan - Missing In Action

TOCABAGA 7: Pàn Guó Zuì - High Treason

TOCABAGA 8: The Invisibles

CONTACT THOMAS H. WARD:

Website: www.ThomasHWardBooks.com
Email: Tocabaga.Jack@gmail.com
Facebook: www.Facebook.com/Tocabaga